A Warchild

Hannah's story

RAGNHILD MUNCK

BALBOA.PRESS
A DIVISION OF HAY HOUSE

Balboa Press books may be ordered through booksellers or by contacting:

Balboa Press
A Division of Hay House
1663 Liberty Drive
Bloomington, IN 47403
www.balboapress.com
844-682-1282

Because of the dynamic nature of the Internet, any web addresses or links contained in this book may have changed since publication and may no longer be valid. The views expressed in this work are solely those of the author and do not necessarily reflect the views of the publisher, and the publisher hereby disclaims any responsibility for them.

The author of this book does not dispense medical advice or prescribe the use of any technique as a form of treatment for physical, emotional, or medical problems without the advice of a physician, either directly or indirectly. The intent of the author is only to offer information of a general nature to help you in your quest for emotional and spiritual well-being. In the event you use any of the information in this book for yourself, which is your constitutional right, the author and the publisher assume no responsibility for your actions.

Any people depicted in stock imagery provided by Getty Images are models, and such images are being used for illustrative purposes only.
Certain stock imagery © Getty Images.

Print information available on the last page.

ISBN: 978-1-9822-4314-2 (sc)
ISBN: 978-1-9822-4315-9 (e)

Balboa Press rev. date: 09/15/2020

Asoul starts its journey on earth by being born into a human body. You could compare it to the wind. No one knows from where it comes and where it goes. On its journey here on earth the soul may encounter infinite possibilities and infinite limitations.

$$\infty$$

More than a hundred years ago a large inn was built on the northern side of a fjord in Denmark, about a hundred yards from the water's edge. The first people to live there would hardly recognize the interior today. But some things have not changed. Through the high windows is a magnificent view over the bay where the fjord has expanded itself. Way out in the horizon the land is no longer visible, as the sea and the sky seem to merge into infinity, while the shores on both sides of the bay sparkle with beauty during the changing seasons. Once in a while the North Sea pushes itself far into the fjord and creates a high tide that almost reaches the foundation of the inn. The people have been known to row in a small boat to the post office half a mile south of the inn to collect the mail, rather than take the flooded road. But that does not happen very often. In wintertime the bay may freeze over and look like the Siberian wilderness, cold and white and barren. But when summer comes with blue skies and sunshine and warm weather the beach swarms with people. The water is wonderfully salty and fresh, and north of the beach is a vast grass field protected against the west wind by forest-clad hillsides.

A long time ago a child was expected here in the old house near the beach. And above the house a soul was hovering, waiting to be born.

$$\infty$$

The day before the child was born, the snow drifted across the land. It poured out of the sky so dense that you could not see your own hand in front of you. The wind took the snow and played with it, blew it up under the roof and into the cracks and corners, threw it around and made the telephone wires sing with it and then got tired for a while, so the snow could settle in drifts before it repeated itself. It was a wild, cold northeaster which gained speed over the fjord and threw itself against the house and made the old inn groan and creak in the joints.

Inside the house it was nice and warm and the lamps were lit already. The innkeeper's young wife sat in a chair and held her arms and hands around her womb with the unborn child. Her long, dark hair was kept in a bun on her head. It framed a face with a finely chiseled nose and large radiant eyes, a mouth with a little Cupid's bow and two delightful dimples in her cheeks. On a rug in front of her played a little girl about two years old, and the woman was humming part of a hymn for her.

"I think it will be soon', she had said to Thomas, before he went out to tend to the animals. "I do not have labor pains yet, but I can feel some twitches. They will probably turn to pains before nightfall"

Then her beloved Thomas had phoned the midwife: "I had better come and get you before it gets dark or we may have to go through this without you. You cannot ride your bicycle in this weather, the snow will soon block the roads."

Thomas went out to help his farmhand in charge of the land and animals belonging to the inn. It took about an hour and a half to milk the cows and feed them and the pigs and the two small fjord horses and close up the stables and barns, so the animals would be safe and warm till next morning.

Gertrud sat and pondered over her marriage of four years. So many wonderful things had happened in her life already. Her older brothers had teased her when she could not hide how much she was in love with Thomas: "You are so young and naive and impulsive. What do you see in that hick?" But her brother Kristian had to swallow his scornful 'hick', when it turned out that Thomas was as wise and kind as he was tall and handsome. And then she and Thomas had married and settled down, and here she was expecting their second child and was serenely happy. Not because they were rich and well known, for they had to watch every penny and be very frugal, but because they were blessed in their daily life together, good and caring to each other. The fishermen and their wives in the fishing village to the south had sized them up a bit when they took over the inn, but they had been accepted with respect for who they were. She was so grateful for Thomas' love and protection and for God's blessing. Thomas was wise and farseeing. If only it would be a boy. Thomas really wanted a son.

She heard the back door open and Thomas stumping to get the snow off his boots. It had gone dark outside while so many thoughts had gone through her mind, and little Bodil had fallen asleep on the blanket at her feet. Gertrud got up quickly from her chair to go and meet Thomas, and at that same moment she felt a contraction shoot through her body and she knew, now it was for real, the baby's birth was near.

She went out to meet Thomas: "You had better fetch the midwife. Now I am sure it is going to be tonight."

Thomas put his arms around her and kissed her: "We have waited almost a month for that little monster, and then what a night to choose to arrive in. Let me eat some supper, then I will telephone doctor Hansen and go and fetch the midwife."

An hour later Thomas drove his new grey Ford into the carriage house, the midwife at his side. She was a round and well proportioned woman, wrapped up to the chin in her scarf and black coat, with a blanket over her knees and her big black bag in her lap. They stomped through the snow over to the house, and Thomas opened the heavy front door. They were met by a wonderful smell of coffee.

The fishermen from the village half a mile south of the inn had been out on the ice to spear eels till it got dark, had then tended to their catch and gone home, each to his little low house. There they were told that the midwife had been seen in the Patron's car. It must be that time with the innkeeper's wife. Why Thomas was called The Patron by the people in the village was a mystery, but it clung to him. In each of the small meticulously clean kitchens a woman waited for her man, if the sea had not already taken him from her. And she fed him well with good food and with questions and answers about things and people. Her questions were answered at suitable intervals in between mouthfuls of food, and she was told that there was more snow on the way and that the wind would increase. One probably would not be able to go out tomorrow as the snowdrifts were already closing the roads.

The winter storm and the darkness came together. The wind

increased and whirled and thundered the snow down in loads. It came howling across the fjord and hurled itself against the houses that stood only a few hundred yards from the edge and had no protection against the wind and the cold.

Ten miles to the west the North Sea roared. It was a good place to be born. Here was dualism for the soul. Here nature could rave wild and unrestricted on a winter's eve. And here it could be mild and enchanting on a summer's night when the fjord was like a mirror between the wood clad shores and phosphorescence sparkled when it dripped from the oars of the boats.

In the old inn by the beach the people were busy. The stove and the fireplaces were tended to and the fire crackled while the wind howled and sang around the corners of the house. The labor pains started that evening and lasted almost till morning.

Then a soul took residence in the girl child that came into the world that January morning. The house seemed to be glowing. It was as warm indoors as it was cold out of doors. There was hot water on the stove and the midwife bossed the maids around in the early hours as the child first saw daylight. And more coffee was brewed.

The storm had put drifts over the ice. The whole bay was an icescape that reminded one of eternal winter in the polar night. As far as you could see there was only snow and ice. Even the few houses on the other side of the fjord were covered in the white blanket. To the east, behind the bay, the sun rose and bathed everything in a radiant light. The sun rose higher and higher above the horizon and lit a light in every little ice crystal till it turned the sky and the white earth into one single blinding white beautiful scene.

The wind had stopped. The air stood still under the sun. The huge snow filled clouds that raced across the sky yesterday had dropped their loads and lay like long, bulging comforters on the hard earth. It was icy cold under the winter sun.

Thomas stood in the warm bedroom where crackling noises came from the fireplace. He looked out over the white snow covered fjord. "Can it be more beautiful anywhere else, do you think?" he said to Gertrud as he turned to the bed where she was resting next to the baby, "but what a cold world for a little girl to come into."

In the kitchen the midwife resided with her coffee cup: "The missus has to stay in bed for ten days," she announced to the kitchen staff and then went on to comment on the awful weather for a midwife to have to go out in, and that for a snip of a girl who should have arrived weeks ago, and who should have been a boy. The Patron himself had come to pick her up and drive her. She was really the most important person at a delivery.

The midwife looked around the kitchen with satisfaction. The young maids here would be needing her themselves some day when their turn came. They might as well be told who would be in charge. The midwife was heavy and big and had a sharp tongue. She wanted respect. When she came to a house to help with a birth it was she who was the boss. Only here it was a little different. The distinguished old doctor from town had come. And The Patron himself could not be bossed around. He was so concerned for his wife with her fine accent. These folks were different. Came from another part of the country and with fine connections. The midwife lorded it at the end of the table. There was strong, black coffee after the hardships in the bedroom. It loosened the vocal chords. And the cook and the waitresses were eager to hear her stories and her talk. Well, if the lass in there had waited much longer she would have half killed her mother, she was so big.

In the bedroom lay the mother with her loosely braided dark hair around her high forehead. Thomas stood looking at her. Her body was as beautiful as the Venus statue, but only he who had just helped their second child into the world knew that.

"Thomas, I think I would like a cup of coffee and a cookie. Imagine, we got another girl. I must write to Mother this afternoon and tell her"!

Thomas smiled at her. "I will get a tray in for you. And with a bun and a soft boiled egg. Then I will drive the midwife home. She is probably ready for that. The roads will soon be cleared. Men are already out shoveling snow."

He left to say about the coffee. Gertrud turned towards the little bed at her side. The newborn was asleep under the comforter. Gertrud lay back in her own pillows. Then she, too, went to sleep.

The child was baptized in the beginning of March. It was an unusually cold winter that year, and it could be difficult to get to the church when the weather was bad. But among the people living north of the fjord the faith in God and the Bible was strong. Nobody wanted to wait too long to have a child baptized. There were some who believed that a soul would be lost and not enter the Kingdom of Heaven, if the child was not baptized. Gertrud was the daughter of a minister and could not really believe this, but it certainly was terribly important to have the child baptized and a very serious situation if a child died before it had received the sign of the cross over its forehead. When Bodil was born, she had been a frail baby and had been baptized at home within two days. Gertrud's second child was robust and strong.

A howling snowstorm raced across the land that Sunday. "You would think little Hannah is protesting her arrival into this world altogether," joked Thomas, "it is a good thing we have 2700."

2700 was the number on the plate of The Patron's grey Ford, the only car in the vicinity. Even if it did not have heat, it was far more comfortable than going by horse and carriage. Mother and child, Bodil and the godmothers, aunt Hannah and aunt Katrina, were given hot bricks under their feet and a big bear skin around them, and the Patron took off with them in the high car with its thin wheels that easily went through a foot of snow. Family members had come from far away, some from Copenhagen and aunt Hannah all the way from Marocco, where she had spent 6 months nursing a French lady. A christening was an important event, and the family was expected to gather when a child was accepted into God's Kingdom

Gertrud was the youngest of 5 siblings and the first to have children, and there was to be a big celebration. The child was named Hannah Katrine after her two godmothers. After the ceremony in church everybody came back to the inn. Boots and coats were shed and people warmed up in the big hall. In the kitchen Dorothea had been busy all morning. She came in from the village to cook when there were big festivities. She was short and round as a ball with her brown hair parted in the middle and a bun perched on top of her head. Some of the guests could not resist sneaking out into the kitchen to shake hands and chat with her till Gertrud appeared and told the guests to come and be seated in the big dining hall. Dinner was ready. The menu was soup with dumplings and meatballs, then roast beef with potatoes, red cabbage, cucumber salad and red current jelly, and for dessert Dorothea's famous rum pudding with strawberry sauce. Uncle Helge had written a song and there were speeches between the courses. It was quite formal.

Back in the kitchen Dorothea and the maids talked about the guests, these fine folks from Copenhagen and other interesting places: "They do talk differently from us, but they are still very nice people," one of them said.

Gertrud had a friend from her Domestic Science College in Copenhagen. She was called Agnes and was born and grew up in Copenhagen. She had been placed next to Gertrud's brother Kristian at the dinner table. Immediately after dessert she came out into the kitchen, praised the food in a loud voice and sported the most scarlet lipstick ever seen in the village. Lipstick was not a common commodity there, and nobody from the village had ever been to Copenhagen.

Dorothea thought Agnes was a marvelous lady. Agnes swept through the kitchen like a whirlwind, talked to everybody, was dressed to the hilt, had well groomed curly hair, made jokes about everything and showed no respect for the fine gentlemen in the dining room. The waitresses had come giggling out into the kitchen telling about Mr. Kristian who had been so flustered and confused over Agnes's jokes at the table that he had poured the strawberry sauce into his wineglass instead of over his pudding. There had been laughter all around the table. There was so much fun in Agnes that everybody at the inn became lighthearted in her presence. Dorothea liked to remember all this during some of the long winter evenings at home. She had lost her husband to the sea and was alone with two sons. One was a fisherman like his father, but the other one brought her shame and sorrow. He could not stay away from his drinking buddies. And of course he could not keep a job that way. It was hard for a mother to watch. But Dorothea forgot that for a while, when Agnes came out in the kitchen and turned the day into laughter. Indeed, it was nice folks who had taken over the inn. Dorothea had been skeptical at first. They were so young and from south of the fjord. But they were church people and worked hard and they brought family and friends to the fishing village from the big world outside. And the Patron's parents and his wife's mother were the nicest people one could wish to meet.

Agnes grabbed a chair and sat down at the kitchen table: "How about a cup of coffee, Dorothea? Let me taste it before you serve it for the guests in there. You must have been standing up for the last three hours. Come and sit down with me for five minutes. The Missus's brother Kristian has not finished your dessert yet. We must let him recover a bit. You know about these men, don't you!"

The maids and waitresses started giggling again. Smiling, round and pleased, Dorothea poured the coffee and sat down.

"You know what, Dorothea, you cannot stay a widow for the rest of your life. Have you taken a good look at the farmhand?"

The christening party continued. And Dorothea came to help out at the inn every time they needed her help, and she became an unforgettable part of the children's lives as did many others who came and went through the doors of the inn.

The two little girls, Bodil and Hannah, were cherished and admired. The Patron loved them dearly and every day he lifted them up in his arms, sometimes way up against the ceiling so they screamed with delight. Everything they did with Father was wonderful. He spoiled them all through their childhood. He gave them sweets when he told them Goodnight. He took them with him to see the cows and pigs and chickens. He held on to them when he lifted them up upon Thor and Odin, the two little fjord horses. And he took them on trips in 2700 where they would sit with straight little backs and look out through the windows till they started teasing each other when the trips got too long.

Mother was their 'umbilical cord' long after their birth. They had been nourished by the milk in her beautiful round breasts. They had fallen asleep in her lap. She was there as a matter of course. She was the warmth and the source they could always return to. She was there like the sea was there, eternal and carrying them forever, as obvious as their own breathing. They did not reflect on it, for that was the only experience they had. Their beds were in the large bedroom where there was a wood stove and a washstand with a jug and a basin, a pail and a chamber pot. They woke up in the morning when Mother and Father woke up.

But one morning the 'umbilical cord' was broken. The world was no longer safe. Something terrible happened. One morning Hannah stood in the middle of the bedroom, a little girl in a long nightie among big furniture and big grownups. She became so scared she remembered the episode from two angles...seen by the little girl on the floor and as a being chased up under the ceiling: She and her parents in the room, her Father holding a chamber pot in front of him and peeing into it, and while she was watching him the thunder that broke lose.

Her mind closed during the stream of words coming from her Mother. "Thomas, how can you stand like that in front of your little girl? That is totally indecent. How can you let her see you like that................."

Hannah remembered nothing else from that morning. She could not share it with anyone, could not ask any questions, for she did not know why her Mother had turned dangerous, why she had shouted at her Father, why she had turned so angry and scary that Hannah just wanted to hide. Mother was no longer warm, caring and loving as a matter of course. She could turn into a shouting monster. She and Father had done something wrong, but she did not know what it was. They were put to shame, but why?

Later in life Hannah sometimes wondered if that episode had caused her Father and herself never to talk intimately about important things in their lives, be it emotions, spirituality or religion. Had a sword of modesty been swung down between them that morning so brutally, that there forever was an invisible barrier in spite of all the love they had for each other. And she wondered if Mother had thrown such a fit because she herself found it repulsive to see her husband pee, but could not say so and instead used the child and the innocence of the child as an excuse to show her anger.

She could have been honest and said: "Thomas, I am such a puritan that it offends me to see you relieve yourself in front of me, please don't do it!" But instead she was moralizing, using the child. That was a kind of lie. As it always was when she didn't give the real reason. And Hannah, later in life, sometimes caught herself using the same pattern, if she did not want to tell the truth, for whatever reason. When she discovered this she would write down the circumstances and look at what she had done and change. She did not want to lie to herself or others.

Gertrud became pregnant again. But she worked too hard. The

guestrooms were occupied all summer. There were well attended meetings with well known speakers coming to stay at the hotel and who attracted hundreds of people to come and hear them speak on the green. There were bathing guests coming to eat in the restaurants at all times of day. And every year in July there was a two-day horse market when more than two thousand horses and people would turn up. Many would come the night before and sleep in the open near their wagons and horses or in tents. Gypsies would come in their painted wagons and vendors would set up shops. Gertrud and Thomas would hire up to sixty extra helpers to serve the many customers on such busy days. Big tents were raised to seat a hundred people for dinner or coffee or beer etc. No Alcohol was served, only light beer.

The busy life at the inn was exciting and rewarding, but also too strenuous. Gertrud had a miscarriage in the middle of summer. The doctor advised her to slow down. The concept of family planning was not mentioned. God blessed a marriage with children. Gertrud would not admit even to herself that it would be a relief not to have to go through childbirth again. And Thomas so much wanted to have a son. He loved his little girls, but a son! He himself had two brothers, he so much hoped for a son.

One day Bodil and Hannah were moved out of the bedroom. For Hannah it was a terrible shock. She was not yet three years old. She cried and protested and had a temper tantrum the first night she was put to bed in a strange room she did not know. It was on the other side of the corridor from the big bedroom, but it was bare and cold. There were just two beds and a washstand. And she was all alone, because Bodil was older and did not have to go to bed as early as Hannah. She cried louder and louder till she finally heard Father's calm voice outside the door:

"Hannah, you have to go to sleep now. We can hear you all over the inn. Good Night!" Somehow that was enough. They could all hear her. And Father was there. She fell asleep.

Then one morning when she wanted to run in to Mother in the big bedroom her Aunt Hannah stopped her: "Wait Hannah, I must talk to you. Come into the sitting-room with me, I have something exciting to tell you!"

Aunt Hannah brought her into the living-room and sat her on the couch next to herself. Aunt Hannah was round and soft and had glasses way down on her crooked nose. She took Hannah's hand and looked down into her little face: "You now have a little brother, Hannah. Mother had a little baby this morning. That is why you cannot go in to see her right now."

Hannah looked straight ahead and wondered: 'A baby, a little baby. What a strange thing." And why should that keep her out of the bedroom away from Mother?

"Mother has a little baby, a little boy," repeated Aunt Hannah, "I will take you in and show you when the midwife has left and he has been washed and wrapped!"

Hannah wondered about this new phenomenon that had to be washed and wrapped.

"Where did he come from?" she asked.

Aunt Hannah sat solidly and pompously on the couch. Solemnly she glanced down her long, crooked nose to the child at her side.

"He came from Heaven," she said, nodding earnestly towards the child, "he has come down from God. And now you have to promise me to stay here and play till I come and fetch you and show him to you."

Aunt Hannah left and walked down the corridor to the bedroom and closed the door after her. Hannah pondered a little while over what she had been told, but not for long. She got down from the couch and tiptoed out of the living room and into the kitchen where the cook and the maids were. They sat at the big table drinking coffee. Hannah could just reach the table with her nose.

"You got a little brother," one of the maids said to her. Hannah looked at her, it was such a weird thing with this baby that all of a sudden was there.

Where did he come from?" she blurted out.

"The midwife brought him," said the maid, "it is the midwife who brings babies."

Hannah said nothing. Now she had been told different things. The grown-ups could not be trusted, and they could be unpleasant. So she kept quiet but wondered. And when she was finally allowed in to see Mother who held a curiously ugly little child, she did not ask where he came from.

Winter came and people at the inn were less busy. But Hannah had lost the sense of safety she had known before. She had lost her place in the big bedroom and she had almost lost Mother. She cried easily and was easily frightened and felt alone and abandoned. She did not know that it was because the new little child made demands on Mother, slept in her lap and took her attention. When she and Father said goodnight to her and would turn the light off, she would cry and say she was afraid of the 'Mourman'. Nobody knew where she had that word from. But to Hannah it was a strange unknown creature, and she could not explain it.

Before Hannah turned three in January she and Bodil were taken to the photographer in town. They were dressed in identical blue dresses with white collars. Bodil was wearing glasses now which made her sweet little round face look even rounder. They were placed on a bench in the studio and told to sit still. Ana's little mouth began to quiver with anxiety. What was going to happen? She was scared. The man in the studio had a big black box on a stand. It pointed directly at her and he dived behind a black piece of cloth to do something horrible. Only when Bodil took her hand and in her protective voice told Hannah that there was nothing to be scared of, did she calm down. When the pictures were delivered she could recognize Bodil, but she did not like to look at the other girl, whom Bodil said was Hannah.

She wanted to be where Bodil was. One day she had a feeling something special was happening. She kept an eye on Bodil who was on her way out to the car. Hannah rushed after her only to be picked up by a couple of strong arms, and then a voice said: "You are staying here with me!"

Hannah howled and screamed and used every fiber in her little body to try to wiggle loose so she could get into the car. Bodil and Mother and Father were getting in. They could not possibly leave without her. Kicking and screaming she was carried into the house by Karen, who stood her up in the window sill so she could look out. That made it worse. She could see her whole family drive away in the car. Without Hannah. How could they? She screamed and kicked. Protesting, wronged and powerless she saw 2700 drive away. It was gone. They had left her.

At long last she let herself be comforted. Karen was there. Karen was going to tell her a story.

Sometimes Hannah and Bodil got into a fight. Bodil wanted to decide everything. Hannah would not always put up with that. When they fought they bit each other. Once Mother called Father and showed him their wrists: "Look how naughty they are, their teeth show in their arms!" Mother kept scolding them: "You should be ashamed of yourselves!" So Hannah learned to be ashamed and bow her head and look down and be quiet, even if she was mad.

If the cook and the maids were not too busy they would allow Hannah to sit with them in the kitchen. She liked that and would often sneak out when she could. They might give her a cookie or something sweet. One day the kitchen maid put her up on the counter top while she was washing the floor. It became a little boring just to sit there, so she opened a cupboard door and looked inside. There were the sugar cubes the grown-ups always put into their coffee cups. She took one and put in in her mouth. At that moment Mother came into the kitchen.

"What are you doing on the counter?" Mother's voice sounded angry and suspicious. Hannah did not answer. It was the maid who had placed her there to get her off the floor. She looked anxiously at Mother and kept her mouth shut. She could not get a word out, she only looked frightened into Mother's eyes.

"Open you mouth. Have you taken sugar?" Hannah's jaws were locked.

"Will you open your mouth!" Mother was angry and squeezed two fingers between Hanna's jaws so it hurt her and she had to open her mouth. There was the sugar cube. Mother took it out.

"You steal sugar! Aren't you ashamed. Get down from there," thundered Mother. Hannah was plumped hard down on the floor. Her mouth hurt. She started crying. She was frightened and humiliated. Mother kept scolding her. Then Father came through the door.

"The child is stealing sugar," Mother's voice cut through the kitchen, "you should be ashamed of yourself, Hannah, shame on you."

Hannah started sobbing. The pain and the shame and the humiliation were too much. Why was Mother angry? Why was it wrong of her to take a lump of sugar. The grown-ups did it all the time. And Mother was telling Father, who said nothing. Hannah was crushed. She ran crying out of the kitchen and started looking for Bodil. And she never forgot. She had done nothing wrong, but Mother punished her.

Her little brother grew bigger and got a name, Kai. He could smile when she stood at his bed and looked at him. Father played with him and bounced him up in the air as he used to to with Hannah.

Now she was too big for that. Kai was the little one, the son, who was made a fuss over. Bodil was the oldest and considered very smart. Hannah often felt left out. She would cling to one or another of the maids when they had time for her. Sometimes she played by herself in the little fenced in yard outside the scullery. She would find flintstones with holes in, put strings through the holes and pretend they were her cows and horses. She would lose herself in her imaginary world. One day she was completely absorbed in her play while sitting on the ground where she got mud and dirt on her clothes.

Then Mother came. The grip on Hannah's arm came as a shock.

"No, au,au!" Hannah screamed and tried to get loose. But the merciless grip on her arm pulled her up. It hurt all the way to the bone. She was pulled through the back door, through the scullery with the cold brick floor. There Mother opened the door to a little room under the staircase. It was very small and there was only a water closet inside.

"Shame on you, you naughty girl. You just got a clean apron, and now it is all muddy. You look like a pigsty. This will teach you. You can sit here till you are good." Mother pushed her into the tiny room that only had a very small window so high up that Hannah could not look out.

Hannah was pushed against the water closet and heard the door being slammed. She stayed on the floor only for a second. Then she got up and started screaming while she pounded on the locked door. She screamed like a wild animal, furious and in pain. Her little hands kept pounding on the door in the darkness and she kept screaming.

Then she heard steps coming back. Mother unlocked the door, pulled her out, slapped her face and pushed her back into the little room.

"How dare you scream like that and bang on the door. I will not come back till you are good!"

Mother's steps vanished, a door was slammed and then stillness. Stillness around her own screams and protests. She was scared, desperate and powerless. She screamed till she got tired and the screams turned into sobbing. Then she became still and noticed the stillness and felt cold on the hard yellow brick floor. Se could only see the yellow bricks, the water closet and the wooden boards in the door. So little light came through the window high above her. She was alone, cold and terrified and her arm hurt.

It was an easy way for Mother to punish. Then she knew where the child was. She had to learn not to get herself dirty. Her will had to be broken. It would not hurt her to sit there for a while.

Perhaps Mother was so busy that she forgot she had left the child there.

But the child did not forget. She tried not to make anybody angry. She tried to be good. Grown-ups were dangerous. It was safest to be quiet and not to be noticed. Only sometimes she did not remember to be careful or she did not know why Mother got angry. Like lightning from a blue sky Mother could be over her and drag her into the little horror chamber. And so in the stillness she would sit there and ponder. She stopped being scared and in a panic. She hated the cold and moist yellow bricks she had to sit on, and the white toilet bowl behind her. Little by little like a plant sprouting in the darkness her anger was born, unarticulated, but keeping her alert and conscious of her surroundings. She would notice when a spider or an earwig ran across the floor and she felt a kinship to them, they were in the same place. Or she would close her eyes and imagine what was outside the door, dream herself away from the little room. She would sit there, a chubby little curlyhead, and fall asleep with a dirty tearstreamed face.

She would wake up to a sharp and commanding voice asking her if she was now a good girl.

But one day her anger and fury rose to the surface. She reacted differently when the condemning voice asked her if she was a good girl.

"No," she screamed. It was not something she had contemplated. It came spontaneously. She had been put into the little dark room once too often. Humiliated and sobbing she had had to say she was sorry and was now a good girl. Not any more.

"No, no, no." There was spite and strength and contempt for consequences in the voice who answered Mother. Se could survive in that little room. Never again would she say yes to being a good little girl.

Mother must have heard the finality and determination in that little voice as a threat. Perhaps Father was nearby. Father would never have let

Mother put her away like that. Or perhaps Mother realized that she had been too strict.

"You had better come out. You need a wash and some clean clothes." she grabbed Hannah's arm and pulled her along into the bedroom. Hannah's whole body was stiff and unwilling. Mother had lost something she would never get back, the unconditional and spontaneous love from her daughter.

Mother washed her face and hands and put her in a clean dress. Mother was impatient and rough and Hannah winced with pain, but kept her face away from her. Father was in the bedroom, playing with Kai, lifting him up in his broad strong hands, and little Kai giggled with delight every time Father had him up near the ceiling. Hannah looked at them. Her face lost its rigidity. She had to laugh with them. Kai's funny round little face was irresistible. And she knew what fun it was to play with Father. Only Father did not play with her any more, because Kai was now the youngest. She did not articulate her disappointment, not even in her mind. She had become the observer instead of the one to be played with. And she laughed with them and shared their joy and became happy again.

Patterns are created in childhood. Mother felt that children should be seen, not heard. Their wills should be broken, so they would become obedient children. "Do as you are told" was her motto, or "Your will is in Father's pocket", and "Quiet when the grown-ups are talking".

It never occurred to Mother that this was a risky way to bring up a sensitive child. Some day a selfish man may take over and demand his ways be obeyed. And the pattern of obedience is already established. Little girls are brought up to be nice and sweet and obedient and the consequence is often a grownup woman who puts up with an abusive husband or sexual harassment. Father had never agreed with Mother's ways. But he was mostly out of the house or busy with people. He would interfere when he heard Mother scold the children or demand something he did not agree with:

"Gentle, gentle with the young colts!" he would say.

Breaking in a young horse to pull a wagon should be done with care and patience. He used that metaphor with children. He loved them and was always fair. But Hannah had to put up with tyranny and abuse and unkind words from Mother while growing up. There were also happy times, but they were not the ones that stood out in Hannah's memory later in life. Mother was too busy and often impatient.

When Kai was born a nursemaid was hired. And Karen came to love Kai and was good towards them all. Fairly often their grandfather would come to visit. He was a big man and quite heavily built with a round, bald head and a warm, lovely smile. He loved to play with the children, would lie down in the grass and let them crawl all over him. Aunt Hannah was another frequent guest who would come and stay on her days off nursing. There were so many people around in the summer time, and often Hannah became a favorite with one of the maids. Then she could be bold and carefree and full of mischief.

All through her childhood Hannah heard verses and stories from the Bible. She remembered them as accompaniment to everything that happened in her life. Most nights when they went to bed, Mother would sit with the children and teach them to say their prayers and tell them that God knows every thought and deed and always watches over everybody.

∽

One day when Hannah was old and sat writing to her daughter, she pondered:

"People sometimes forget and rush ahead in rage and impatience. And the child...the child they once carried tenderly in their arms and considered their most precious treasure …. that child they now thunder against and wipe out the love in the eyes of the child, and it is replaced with anger and contempt. Our hour of visitation is while the child is with us, in our care. Some day the child is grown and gone. Does the child hate us or love us or have ambiguous emotions? One day it may be too late for us! We may have lost what we loved the most. Perhaps we offended one of 'His little children'. And it says in the Bible that it would be better if we were lowered to the bottom of the sea with a millstone around our neck than to offend one of 'His little ones.' Do we pay so dearly for offending a child?...

'Jerusalem, Jerusalem, if only you knew the hour of visitation! If only you knew on this day what would serve you. But it is hidden from your eyes. And days will come....'

※

When Hannah was four years old Mother took her and Bodil on a long trip by train and ferries to visit Aunt Inger and Uncle Niels, The children were very excited and Mother was kind and loving and relaxed and read Hans Christian Andersen's stories while they traveled across Fuhnen where he was born.

Uncle Niels met them at the station, and Aunt Inger had coffee and juice and cakes for them at home. There were so many knick-knacks in the home and so many flowers in the garden, so much to see that was new to the girls. It was all very exciting. They slept the moment they were put to bed, tired after the long journey and the newness of it all. Bodil woke up first:

"Wake up, wake up!" she kept saying to Hannah who slowly opened her eyes to look around in this new strange place. And Mother opened the door and smiled happily to her little girls:

"Good morning, good morning, ready to get up?" and she helped them get dressed and ready for breakfast.

Uncle Niels met them with big smiles and hugs: "How wonderful to have two beautiful girls visit us. We will have a lot of fun things to do today.!"

He and Inger had no children of their own and he enjoyed playing with them. After breakfast Hannah sat in the sofa and read a book when suddenly a horrible noise startled her. She saw aunt Inger push a very weird thing towards her. It made more noise than a train and a barking dog together, or at least Hannah thought so. It came closer and closer. Terrified Hannah jumped up from her seat and hid behind the sofa, her eyes big as teacups with fear.

"Don't be a little fool. It is just a vacuum cleaner. Big girls are not afraid of it."

Aunt Inger's voice had a bit of contempt in it as she kept pushing the vacuum cleaner closer and closer. But Hannah was terrified until Mother came and rescued her and took her and Bodil for a walk. When they traveled back home to the inn they crossed a new bridge just opened. And at home everybody talked about the new bridge and were not interested in hearing about the scary, noisy vacuum cleaner. But Hannah never forgot and she never again felt at ease with aunt Inger.

It only took three hours for Father to drive from the inn to Mother's mother whom they called Nana. She lived on a big farm You came through a large gateway in the old barn and into a farmyard surrounded by buildings that created a huge square area. Attached to the barn was on one side a huge cowshed, on the other a stable for horses and a large pigsty. Coming through the gate you saw in front of you the large main house which had a horseshoe shape. Nana had her living quarters in the middle. The left wing contained a large kitchen and dining room and larders, the right wing had an office and laundry quarters, etc.

When you came into Nana's big sitting room it was somewhat gloomy. The walls had a brownish color, and Hannah had once called it poop colored, which had prompted Mother to tell her to go into the corner, stand there and be ashamed... "and don't look around!"...so she did not comment on it any further.

Nana was small and round and very old. She had a little round head with thin white hair. In her large sitting room was a brown grandfather clock as old as the house. And there was a large round mahogany table in the middle of the room, sofas along the walls and a big grand piano near the windows towards the park. There was a door leading into a sunroom on one side and a door leading into her bedroom on the other side and another door leading into a small private dining room. In the living room hung a large photograph of Mother's father. It showed a stern man with a very large moustache. But Hannah was not going to comment on that so as not to get in trouble. She preferred to be in the sun room if they were not outdoors. That was where Nana had her desk and chair on a raised platform. From there she had a view down the long Chestnut avenue stretching all the way to the Swan Lake. From the sun room you could see the whole park with its big lawns and flowerbeds and the pergola covered with roses. The avenue was for walking only, not cars or carriages. The grown-ups would walk steadily and slowly and the children dash off in all directions. There were so many things to see but most interesting was a little thatched hut within an enclosure. In there were gold pheasants and bantams and sometimes a peacock on eggs or with her little chicks, to protect them from the fox. Mostly the peacocks walked around freely in the park. They made funny shrieking sounds, but were perfectly harmless.

When Bodil and Hannah came to visit Nana they often sat with her in the sun room and listened to the stories she would read to them. She would also show them how to crochet and knit. Once the story was so exciting that Hannah would not interrupt to get help with her crocheting. She just sat there and moved her hands as if she was doing it, till Nana looked at her and started laughing. That was quite embarrassing, but Nana never scolded her, just showed her. She had two ladies helping her in the house. Andrea was soft and nice and helpful, but aunt Max as they had to call her was not popular. She was tall and bony with grey hair and sharp features and looked like the witch in one of their books. When Hannah and Bodil sat down for breakfast aunt Max said they could either have honey on their bread or sugar in their tea, but not both, for there was no reason for indulgence. Her voice was loud and jarring and she constantly told them: "Sit up straight. No elbows on the table. Finish what is on you plate." etc.

When Kai was almost a year old Father and Mother brought the three children down to Nana to stay for three weeks. With them came Karen who was going to look after all three of them while Father and Mother went await to visit Bruxelles and Paris and London. Karen loved Kai as if he were her own, and she gave him cream to drink instead of milk, so he grew fatter and fatter and had the loveliest dimples in his cheeks. When they first walked in the park, Karen insisted the girls stay close to her. There was a sinister looking man, nicknamed 'the Pirate' walking around and raking the many pathways.

"You have to stay close to me. Don't talk to him. He could get angry. Perhaps he eats small children," Karen warned them.

Bodil became quite indignant over such nonsense: "He never hurts anybody. He is always here when we come. Nana always lets us run around on our own in the park. That's what we want to do." And after a few days Karen stopped being nervous.

Nana was always helpful and had many people come to see her. And whenever a pig or calf was slaughtered on the farm, Nana would make sure some of the meat was given to people she thought might appreciate it. She would sometimes say: "We Christians are no better than other people, but we feel better, we are happier, we are here to help those less fortunate than us."

Hannah was so happy with Nana that she did not want to leave, but one day Mother and Father came back, and that was wonderful. Kai had learned to walk a few steps by himself, so they were very impressed. Hannah felt so proud on his behalf.

One day home at the inn when Bodil and Hannah were very sick with Measles, Mother told them that Nana had fallen ill. She and Father had to go and be with her. Anine, their trusted helper from the village, would stay with them and care for them. The curtains in the bedroom were drawn to protect their eyes, said Anine, when Bodil complained. Hannah did not mind, she was so miserable, she just wanted to sleep. And when Mother and Father came back home they told them that Nana had died. Now they would no longer go and visit her on the farm. That was so sad and strange.

Sometimes the summer guests at the inn talked to the children, who were told never to approach them or disturb them. But one summer the lady in Room 5 invited Hannah into her room. Hannah went a little reluctantly, for the lady was wearing bright red lipstick, something Mother did not approve of. But the lady made Hannah feel very comfortable, showed her things and asked her questions, as if she were a grown-up, and Hannah felt quite important in her company.

"You are so lucky to live here," said the lady and lifted her up on a chair, so she could look out over the fjord, "look at the fjord, how blue it is. And see the coastlines on both sides of the bay, how lovely with the bushes and trees growing there, and right out there in front of us you can not see land. We don't know what is there. It is fascinating when sea and sky meet. Then there is something that pulls at us to find out. What is beyond this invisible border? Some day you will be a grown-up and want to travel and find out. This is one of the most beautiful places on earth. That is why I come here every year. When you grow up and travel out into the world, you will always want to come back and visit this place."

The lady made Hannah look at the fjord in a way she had never done before. It used to be there as a matter of course. Now it had become special, something beautiful that belonged to her because she lived here.

She had a new friend who taught her to appreciate nature. But one day the lady left and went back to Copenhagen.

It became a conscious joy for Hannah on a summer morning to leave the house and look at the fjord when it was calm as a mirror, framed by green clad cliffs and hills. She loved being outdoors, alone on the beach. She would feel the sand between her toes, take a handful and let it trickle through her fingers. She would pick up snails and shells and seaweed. She was so much a part of this world, of earth and roots and worms, sticklebacks and fish. Her world grew bigger, as she grew older and dared walk further away from the house. She knew the horses and cows in the stable, she knew which sows to stay away from, which of them could be dangerous. She learned respect for the West wind which could drive a boat away from the shore. Once in a while Father would close his big hand around her smaller one and take her out in the fields, perhaps show her how to pull up a carrot, wipe it clean with the green top and eat it right there. She loved being with Father.

But she did not understand Mother, who said she loved her children, but could be so angry and scary. One morning, when she woke up Mother would shame her and tell her never to touch herself between her legs. Hannah had no idea what she was talking about, so Mother explained that it was bad to have her hands between her legs when she went to bed. No other explanation. Hannah felt spite and anger, she was being accused of something she had no idea about. Her soul protested, her face closed up. Mother demanded obedience. Her body belonged to Mother, who could punish any way she wanted. But now Hannah had a weapon. If she was angry with Mother she could place her hands where she was not supposed to and pretend she was asleep, if Mother checked on her. There were episodes that made Hannah hate Mother. But she never complained to Father, or to anybody. That for whatever reason was unthinkable. It never occurred to her.

And Mother's way of bringing up her children? Was it just one long emotional reaction to her own situation, circumstances she did not know how to change? Was the job of running the inn so demanding, that the children were a constant nuisance if they got in her way or did something that displeased her? And her temper so hot she could not be rational? Hannah tried to be obedient, to stay out of trouble, never to talk back.

One day she sat outdoors in the grass and looked down into a large Queen Anne's Lace flowerhead. Insects were busy crawling around inside it, fascinating to watch. It was their house, their world. She was so engaged in keeping an eye on the small creatures that she did not notice she had got dirt on her apron. Suddenly Mother was there.

"Look at you, child. We just gave you a clean apron. Look how dirty you already are. Get up!"

Hannah's whole body grew stiff, her eyes big and scared and the little mouth started to quiver. Mother had pulled her up with a hard grip around her arm.

"Look at me!" Mother's hand grasped her chin with merciless force and her jaw opened. She started to cry. Mother's eyes pierced angrily into hers and paralyzed her soul. There was nothing she could do. It never occurred to her to scream or get hysterical. She did not dare do anything for fear of Mother, who said Aunt Inger and Uncle Niels were on their way and she should have kept her apron clean. She tried to sink down to get free of Mother.

"Stay where you are while I am talking to you! If you cannot behave yourself, you can go to bed for the rest of the day." A hard grip on Hannah's arm made her wince.

"What is going on here?" suddenly Father was there, and Mother let her go.

"Look how she has made herself dirty. She just had a clean dress and apron."

Hannah looked up at Father while she tried to pull away her hurting arm.

"Then let her be a little dirty. We live in the country. It is perfectly normal for a little girl to get dirty." Father sounded impatient.

"Thomas, we are expecting guests. I want our little girls to look clean and neat." Mother's face took on a look of resentment.

"O.K., O.K. Let us go inside and worry about more important things."

Father took Mother's arm and steered her up the stairs and in through the door.

Hannah saw them go. Her arm still hurt, and her cheeks were wet with tears. She felt lonely and wronged. Father and Mother belonged together, but Father had saved her. It automatically went on his credit side on his non-existing balance sheet.

Then she heard a car coming. She pressed herself against the wall. The car stopped and out came uncle Niels and aunt Inger. They immediately saw Hannah.

"Come and get a hug from Uncle Niels. How you have grown. But what is this? Have you cried? Are you crying because we come to visit you?" Uncle Niels tried to look surprised.

That brought a little smile on Hannah's face. And while her arm still hurt, she took Uncle's hand and looked up into his smiling eyes. Aunt Inger came and gave her a hug and said, "How big you are. We have not seen you since Christmas! We have brought something for you and Bodil. Lets go and say Hello and then open the present."

She went into the house with them. Big Welcome and lots of talk. Mother had coffee ready for them. Hannah stood and listened while Aunt Inger brought a little packet out of her big purse and told Bodil and Hannah to open it. There were the most beautiful little bows and lace collars, and Bodil and Hannah said 'Ah' and 'Ih' and 'Oh', how lovely.' And Aunt Inger showed them to Mother who said in a somewhat tart voice that she tried to bring up her girls to be modest, not to be vain. It was enough if they were clean and neat.

Hannah and Bodil looked at Aunt Inger and back at Mother. It was Mother who decided, but Aunt Inger would always give her opinion.

"Gertrud, You must be going to a party once in a while at Christmas time and dress up. Your husband always looks very nice. It is not a luxury to wear a white collar and velvet bow over a woolen dress. I really thought you would appreciate my gifts yo your little girls."

Thank you, but we do not need any luxury", Mother said, "and now let us hear your news."

Hannah stole out of the room. Mother was not in a pleasant mood. But Uncle Niels caught up with her and asked what she suggested they play now. Bodil joined them and together they went down to the beach and started building sand castles. Then aunt Inger turned up and suggested she teach Hannah to swim properly. She did not protest, but her own way of swimming was much faster. She used one arm as an arrow and the other as an oar and shot through the water. She could not remember not being able to swim.

One Sunday morning Bodil woke up early and went over to Hannah's bed, grabbed her arm and said: "Wake up, we are going down to Mom and Dad!" Ana stumbled after her down the two steps from their little bedroom into the big bedroom, where Mother and Father were still asleep.

"Good Morning!" Bodil announced their arrival in a loud voice, and Mother and Father woke up and made room for their two girls in their big four poster bed. The round face of Kai, who was barely two, appeared at the foot of the bed, where his cot was: 'Me too, Me too' he said. He managed to get out of his diaper and crawl up to the head of the bed, where he staggered for a moment, then lost his balance and planted his fat little fanny right on top of Mother's face, from where he was very quickly lifted away.

Bodil and Hannah laughed so much their tummies hurt, and Mother could not help laughing either. It was such a lovely Sunday morning in October when Father and Mother had time to spend with their three kids. During summer months they were much too busy at the inn to do much of anything with their children.

Mother talked with Father about Sunday school, now the two girls were big enough to join. So one day they went up to an old and tired looking little house above the hill. There was no grass, no bushes outside, just barren ground. The walls needed whitewashing and the front door needed paint. Once inside they were introduced to the Sunday School teacher. They had to curtsy and say their names. He showed them where to sit, among a group of other children. Hannah looked at the wooden floor and the benches which looked so worn and old. The walls were whitewashed and there were no pictures, only a cross behind the teacher's chair. On the cross hang Jesus with his head drooping and a nasty wreath of thorns around his head. There was nothing inviting about this place.

The teacher started saying a prayer. Hannah folded her hands the way Mother had shown her to do when praying, and she bent her head. But not for long. She could not help but take a peep at the other children to see if they were doing the same. She thought about her hands. It was really strange that one should fold one's hands in a certain way and look serious. Then the teacher began singing a hymn which Hannah knew from home, but she did not think the teacher sounded very nice. She looked at her hands and noticed the knuckles and the lines and she forgot to listen. Then Bodil hissed at her to sit still. She had not noticed that she sat kicking with her legs. She looked around at the other children. Most sat like herself with rounded backs and looked at the teacher. She noticed a little boy who sat up straight and she immediately did the same. She remembered Mother often told them to sit up straight and not look like a bow.

Then the teacher began telling the story about the farmer who started spreading grain, and some fell in good soil and some on the road and some among thistles. This was a good story. Hannah could see it all in her mind. She knew thistles and roads. And Father sometimes talked about good soil and poor soil. And the teacher explained that sometimes people remembered God's words. Sometimes they only remembered for a short while and sometimes not at all. For there were people who were cold and hard like the roads, so the grain could not sprout there. Hannah understood it all. It was a good story. And she felt she knew Jesus quite well. You could trust him like you could trust Father.

And then the big day came when there was to be a Christmas party at the Sunday School. Oh, the tree was the biggest Hannah had ever seen. It was bigger than Father. The dull room was completely changed. There were decorations everywhere. And tables with plates and cups and glasses and cookies and lemonade and coffee.

The teacher read the Christmas story about Jesus being born. They sang Christmas carols and they all walked around the tree many times. Now Hannah knew all the children and looked in wonder at their parents. The women had their hair in a bun on their heads just like Mother, the men had such big hands and their hair looked wet. After singing more carols the teacher read a story about three children without father and mother and how they walked in a snowstorm and almost missed Christmas, but were saved by some nice grown-ups in the last minute.

After the story the children were given each a little bag with sweets and an apple, Hannah sat and enjoyed it while watching the candles on the tree. When she squeezed her eyes tight, the flame on a candle seemed almost round, and she dreamed herself away into the story about

Jesus. She saw the crib, where they had laid the baby. She remembered the fragrance of fresh hay, and how lovely it smelt of milk, when she put her nose against the neck of the red cow in the cowshed. She loved the smell in the stable and the sounds and the cosiness when coming in from outside and hear the animals munching. Nowhere did she feel safer that with the animals. That was a good place to be born.. And imagine, the angels sang outside in the fields. And there were shepherds outside looking after their sheep that time of year. No wonder they hurried back home from the fields and into the stable, when they were told that Jesus had been born.

"Hannah is getting sleepy," she suddenly heard Mother say up above her head, "it is time to go home Hannah. Father thinks it is time to go home."

When Father said something, one always did it. And when Mother said that something was God's command or that Father wanted it, one never objected. Hannah would have wanted to stay longer to see the tree and the candles, did not want to miss a single moment of the Christmas party. She just looked silently at Mother and her eyes said all that her thoughts could not form and her mouth not say. And then she heard Bodil say it:

"Oh, Father can't we stay a little longer?" she pulled at his sleeve. Father had his back to her and was talking with the teacher. He turned around.

"Sure, we do not need to go yet. We can wait till the candles have burned down.

"Hurray", shouted Bodil and danced away. Hannah's face became one big smile. For an instant the thought about Mother went through her head. How strange that Mother had said that Father wanted them to go home, when he had just said they could stay. But then she chased after Bodil and they played till the candles burned down and the electric light came on.

The room again became the worn old place with the wooden benches and the grey, dusty floor. The magic was gone, the spell was broken. There was no longer a baby Jesus, no angels or shepherds, no singing, no joy. It had been a wonderful evening. Suddenly it was over. How strange.

She looked around to find Father and hurried over to go home with him and Mother and Bodil.

∞

The old inn was built in red brick with the tall windows facing the fjord, so close to the water's edge that you could throw a stone from the front steps and hit the water. Coming out of the heavy front door and walking along the beach to the right you would come to a harbor from where a small ferry crossed over to a large island. The little fishing village had no more than a hundred houses, a post office and a grocery store. The little ferry had room for only four cars plus bicycles and passengers. A heavy beam was placed on both ends, so cars would not roll overboard. But the children knew that before they were born one old man had been so nervous driving on to the ferry that he had not put his brakes on in time. His car hit the beam and plunged into the harbor. It was a terrifying thought and whenever they were on the ferry they kept close to the side railings. Still it was exciting to be far out on the fjord.

When Father went to the grocery store, the children wanted to go with him. They loved all the smells in the little store, from spices and ropes and tar and herrings in large barrels. And the fat little grocer with his round smiling face would always end the order by putting hard candy in a cone he made of paper. The moment they were out of the door they had a piece of candy.

When you walked to the left out of the inn you came to the large grass field where people flocked in the summer time to sunbathe and swim in the fjord. Father built a kiosk at the entrance to the field and Ellen, a lady from the village, worked there to sell ice cream and chocolate and other goodies. Ellen was a tiny lady with a pronounced hunchback. She was smart and quick and fair and she would give the children whatever might be broken and could not be sold.

Sometimes the children were punished for things they knew they should not have done. But punishment only made Hannah more cautious. She never accepted Mother's punishment as just, because it was always humiliating. Farther never punished the children, he explained why it was not smart to do this or that and why. Then they felt as if they were his coworkers or conspirators because he had treated them with respect and shared his reasons and viewpoints. He was never unreasonable.

Running a seaside hotel was a lot of work in the summer. Thomas and Gertrud would be up 6 o'clock in the morning and often not get to bed till almost midnight. Gertrud's quick temper and no doubt her busy lifestyle contributed to her anger when she became irritated with the children. She had another miscarriage. But a year later a little girl was born, so now there were four.

Hannah remembered one particular day when all four children had displeased Mother. She told them to stay in the bedroom while she called Father. They sat on the huge fourposter bed and waited with solemn faces. When Father came in through the door Mother immediately began telling him about their behavior. They had all been so naughty, she said.

When she had finished Father said very slowly: "I think the five of you are equally naughty."

For Hannah the world stood still. That anybody would dare say that to Mother was asking for a 'vulcanic eruption'. At least it would have been if anybody but Father had said it. Gertrud dearly loved Thomas and he was probably the only person she could not boss around. She never summoned him again to scold the children. Perhaps she felt he was unjust not to support her, but he would not punish them.

On the top shelf in one of the closets in the bedroom, Father kept boxes of chocolate and other goodies. And every evening when he came to say goodnight he brought each child a small piece of chocolate. He never smoked, but he was fond of chocolate and loved to share. The children never forgot.

As often as possible Mother and Father would attend church on Sundays, and when Bodil and Hannah were old enough to sit still they came with them. They wore their best dresses and were told to curtsy to the Parson and his wife. The Parson was always kind, took Hannah's hand and talked to her and made Hannah feel important. One Sunday Bodil and Hannah sat on the bench behind Mother and Father. Hannah was given a hymnbook and immediately dropped it on the floor. She got a stern look from Mother and she looked around to see if anybody else had heard the bump. All the women were wearing hats on heir heads, the hair in a bun at the back of the neck.

Hannah tried to read the hymn Bodil showed her they were to sing, but she gave up. It was nothing like the rhymes in her books at home, the ones she knew by heart. Just before the parson was to go up into the pulpit Mother turned around and whispered to Hannah: "Now, remember to sit still and listen!" And she sat very still and tried to understand what the Parson was talking about. She did not always understand and her thoughts would wander off. But then she heard a new word, she had never heard before. The Parson emphasized the word hypocrite and went on to explain. He told about the Pharisee and the Publican so vividly that Hannah felt she could see them in her mind, how the Pharisee stood erect and proud near the entrance of the synagogue with his face turned up, thanking God because he was not like the poor Publican further down who was wringing his hands and asking forgiveness for his sins. The Parson talked about the hypocrisy and explained it with examples. Hannah learned a new word. She looked around at everybody.

"I have to remember it," she thought, "I am five years old and I have learned what hypocrisy is. It is important. I am sitting on the bench behind Mother and can see, that she is nodding at everything the Parson says. None of the other ladies do that." Hannah turned around to check on all the other ladies in church. Yes, her mother was the only lady who sat tight lipped and nodded at everything the Parson said.

"My Mother is a hypocrite," Hannah ascertained, "She is sitting there showing everyone else that she agrees with the Parson. It is almost, as if she had something in common with him that the others have not. She is like the Pharisee. She is not pious at all. I know Mother. She can be mad and unjust. She can smile and speak nicely to strange people, and they have no idea how terrible she can yell and slap and pinch. It is hypocrisy, when she is sitting there, nodding at everything, the Parson says."

Hannah kept looking at Mother and the other ladies. "I have to remember this till I am a grown-up. I must remember, that when I was five years old, I learned what it is to be a hypocrite and that I knew my Mother is a hypocrite. I must remember, so when I have children I will not be a hypocrite."

For of course one had children when one became a grownup.

One day Hannah woke up feeling miserable. She felt hot and her arms were itching. When she looked at them they were red and swollen. When Mother saw her she called the doctor who took one look at her and said she probably had Scarlet Fever. She would have to go to the hospital. And while Hannah said she did not want to go anywhere, she was taken to the hospital and placed in a room all by herself. The room had shiny green walls and there was a strange smell in the room. There was only a bed, a nightstand and a chair in the room. The bed was made of metal and was white and cold to touch. She did not have an eiderdown, only a blanket. It was very uncomfortable just to have a blanket that was tucked tightly under the mattress. Hannah tried to pull it up so it could be snug around her shoulders like her eiderdown, but it just was not the same. The nurse who had brought her into the room said she would be back soon, but she was not. Hannah lay in the bed feeling more and more lonely and afraid and unhappy. Nobody came and there was nothing to do. She did not have a book or anything to look at, only the green walls and the ceiling. She cried herself to sleep.

She woke up when a nurse came in with a tray. There was steamed codfish, boiled potatoes with a little butter and a glass of milk. The nurse put it down on the white chair next to the bed and asked Hannah how she was doing. Hannah was a little scared of her as she stood there in her white, starched uniform with a cap on her head and looked very stern and impatient. "My head hurts," she said, "and I am not hungry." she had taken one look at the food on the plate and decided she did not want any of that. It looked terribly uninteresting in all its pale likeness to everything else in the room.

"Try to eat something!" said the starched uniform, "it is especially for children with a temperature like the one you have. And tomorrow we may find out if you have Scarlett Fever. If you do you can be moved into a ward with other children"

Red and swollen and miserable she dosed off to sleep again. She spent the night and all next day alone in the green and white room. For breakfast they brought her oatmeal with milk and sugar. Hannah took one spoonful of the grayish white stuff and made a funny face. It was drowned in sugar, horribly sweet, no way could she eat that. Again the food was left on the tray and taken out again by a female in something white and starched.

Hannah slept and cried, slept and cried. Why did no one come to see her? Why did she not get something to read? She felt totally abandoned. She discovered a little spider next to the windowsill. It was busy making a cobweb. Suddenly it dropped all the way down to the floor and crawled across the gray and white linoleum towards her bed. Hannah rolled over on her side so she could keep and eye on the spider. It reached the foot of the bed. Hannah put a hand on the cold metal and bent over the side to keep an eye on it. But it disappeared behind the wheel of the bed. She fell back on her pillow and felt sorry. It would have been nice to keep watching another live creature in the room, empty of all humanity. For two whole days she was there alone. Once in a while a starched uniform would come in with steamed fish and mashed potatoes or porridge with too much sugar on top. Hannah would have none of it. She took one look at the food and turned away. The white uniform did not even give her a book or magazine to look at, or stayed and talked with her little bit.

After two days a doctor came and said she could be moved into a ward with other patients. She walked in slippers and nightgown into the big ward. There were eight beds in a row. At first she just stood still and looked, then a voice from one of the beds called out:

"Hannah, here we are. Come and join us. Look, there is your sister next to me."

Hannah's spirit rose almost to the ceiling. Hurray, there was Bodil and there were Mary and Lilian and Ida and Johanna. What a relief and what a surprise to see Bodil and four maids from the inn. They chatted and had fun and said it was terrible for her parents that most of their help were sick so they had no help at the inn. Bodil peeped out from under her cover: "I am not feeling very well! We all came in yesterday!"

Hannah started feeling much better now she had company. But they all had to stay six weeks in the hospital. That was horrible. And it was almost strange to come home after such a long time away. Mother looked at her two girls and said their hair looked dull, they should have a haircut. So their braids came off. That afternoon Hannah tiptoed into the bedroom where her parents were having their afternoon nap. She wanted to look at herself in the large bedroom mirror. She thought she looked quite pretty. Father saw her and laughed quietly while pointing her out to Mother:

"Look at her! I think she is beginning to become a little lady. She is interested in her new hairdo!"

Bodil had been frail from birth and Father did not want her to walk the long way to the local school. It would have meant walking more than a mile and uphill every morning early, and a long walk home again. So when she was seven years old a young woman called Meili came to the inn to be her teacher. Meili was born in China where her parents had been missionaries, but now her father was a parson in a nearby parish. She was a lovely and well educated girl, nineteen years old. Hannah wanted to join them every morning to listen to the lessons, and soon she was given a pencil in hand and told she could start practicing writing letters and numbers. After the lessons Meili would sit on the couch in the room with a child on each side of her and read a story or nursery rhymes. It was not long before Hannah knew the rhymes by heart and one day while Meili was reading Hannah suddenly exclaimed:

"Meili, I can read, listen, I recognize it all. I can read." She recognized the words.

For two years Meili stayed with them, then she married a nice man in the nearest town. But by then both girls had learned so well, that when they were tested in the local school as all home schooled children had to be, they were both praised by the examiner. Then Bodil started riding on a bus to the school in town and Hannah was to start at the local school. She was strong and tall for her age. She walked to the little house where she had gone to Sunday school and sat on the grey benches with other kids her age. She was easily bored. She could read fluently any text, while Nora, the girl sitting next to her slowly spelled every word before pronouncing it. It was totally boring.

But Hannah made a friend, Edith, whom she met walking home from school. Edith lived half a mile from the school on a farm on the hill above the meadow and with a view over the inn and the fjord beyond. Edith was limping and could only walk slowly and said she was so happy that Hannah would walk with her: Would she stop at her house and come and meet her mother. Edith's mother greeted her with kindness and enthusiasm: "Are you from the inn? How nice of you to walk with Edith, come and have tea and a cookie before you go on." Hannah was so impressed. She was greeted as her parents were when they were visiting others. Hannah was not used to being greeted as someone special. It felt good. But she missed Meili and did not much care for the local school. She learned about inches and centimeters. At least that was new to her. And she quickly learned to use the local dialect, the one also spoken by most of the helpers at the inn, but not by Mother. Mother was born near Copenhagen and when Hannah came home from school and spoke the local dialect she was told to 'speak properly'!

✺

On a day in April, 1940, Hannah was standing outside the inn next to Father and Kasper, the farmhand, looking up into the sky.

"Look, look there – can you see the aeroplanes? They are flying right over us. They are on their way to Norway!"

Father was pointing up in the sky. The only thing Hannah saw was three sparrows sitting on a telephone wire. She just could not see any aeroplanes. In front of her the fjord was calm and peaceful. But Father was upset. He said the war had broken out. She saw tears running down his cheek. She did not know a man could cry. Something terrible had happened. She heard him say to Kasper: "This is shameful, shameful, and now Norway!"

Father's words resonated with Hannah. She understood that the grownups had to be ashamed. It was a feeling she knew all too well. If she had been nosy or done something wrong or just been in the way, Mother would tell her to be ashamed.

"Aren't you ashamed?" Mother might yell, "Look at me. You should be ashamed of yourself!" and then she had to look into Mother's graygreen eyes that seemed to penetrate her soul and read her thoughts.

But now she heard Father say that the grownups should be ashamed because German soldiers had been able to march into Denmark. Father had been a soldier when he was young. She had seen his handsome blue uniform in a closet. It was a good thing he was no longer a soldier and could be shot in a war. But he felt betrayed. He felt there were people who had betrayed Denmark and that the soldiers should have put up more of a fight against the invaders. That the country should have been more prepared against the enemy from the south. Now he had just pointed out their aeroplanes coming from the south, flying north towards Norway.

For a while the war changed nothing at the inn. Bodil had started school in town and took the bus every day. Hannah walked to the little country school. The grownups talked about war but nothing much seemed different. Kai was no longer the youngest child, there was the new little sister. So one day Kai was moved up to sleep in the same room as Bodil and Hannah. A bunk bed had been installed and they sometimes took turns playing in the upper and lower bed. Some days they would hang a blanket down from the upper bed and pretend they had a cave and many secrets. One day when Kai was in the upper bed, he asked Hannah if she could bump him up and down by pushing her feet up against his mattress. It became a hilarious game and they took turns bumping each other till Kai suggested Hannah should see if she could bump him out.

"Of course I cannot bump you out when you hold on to the sides of the bed", she said. Kai could be quite generous. He folded his hands over his stomach and shouted: "Go ahead, see if you can!"

Hannah was lying in the lower bed with her legs straight up in the air. She bent them a little bit and then pushed up with all her might, hitting the mattress just under Kai's backside. He flew in half a circle out of the bed and hit the wash basin at the opposite wall. The noise was incredible. Kai and the wash basin landed together on the floor. Laughter turned into howling. The door flew open and Mother appeared.

"What on earth are you doing? Hannah, you should know better. Shame on you. You could have killed him. Go to sleep immediately."

Now they could not play that game anymore. Kai had stopped howling. "I did not really hurt myself, I just go a little scared," he said. And so they just whispered together till they fell asleep.

One day a policeman turned up and told Father that he had to house a unit of German soldiers. Father refused but was told he did not have a choice. The German Wermacht took whatever they wanted. And they wanted a small unit of soldiers stationed there. Father owned a house next to the inn, so that became their quarters and none had to stay in any of the hotel rooms. Father told the children never to talk to the soldiers, not even look at them or come near them. They should be careful about their coming and going so as not to be approached by any soldier. And Ana heard Father and Mother talk about the time ahead. It would be dangerous and they all had to be careful about what they said and did. The children understood and kept their distance.

Father used to buy large quantities of coffee and tea and cocoa and chocolate to use and sell at the inn. When the war broke out he bought extras of everything, knowing there would be a shortage and rationing till the war was over.

When summer came the inn had many guests from Copenhagen as usual. And on beautiful days the beach would team with people and business was good.

They did not see much of the soldiers.

One Sunday morning Hannah was up early and went outside. The fjord was dark blue and a warm southern wind seemed to be pushing white clouds in the sky and white sails on the water as if they were racing each other. She was 9 years old and out of school for the summer and could do what she wanted, never mind the grownups.

She walked slowly down to the water's edge. She wanted to collect shells and little flintstones with holes in so she and Kai could tie strings through the holes and pretend they were playing with farm animals.

The fjord was calm near the shore. She picked up a flat stone and sent it skipping across the water surface and smiled with satisfaction. 10-12 times it skipped. Nor bad. She bent down to look at things in the water. There were jellyfish, starfish and sticklebacks and little crabs frantically scamping sideways on the bottom, and there were some nice shiny little pebbles. There was only a ripple up against the shoreline, tiny little lapping waves creating a soothing, calming sound. Bending further down to watch the life under water one of her golden brown pigtails slid off her shoulder and a stickleback snapped at her pigtail. She laughed inside but didn't move. She did not want to disturb the life down there.

"It must be fun to be God," she thought, "he is able to stand just like me and look down on the whole world under him. And if he wants to, he can mess it up just as I can if I move my pigtail around."

She stood still as a mouse till she got tired in her back from bending over to observe the world beneath her. She was part of this world, was nurtured by the fruits of the soil and the sea. She felt at one with it, had secrets with it that no one else knew about. When she swam in the fjord with her eyes wide open under water she could see patterns in the sand, made by worms and busy little crabs, and they sometimes made her laugh so she had to get up for air.

She skipped further along the beach where the sand met the grass and where the huge grassy field was open to beachgoers. At the end of the green the broad beach shrank to a narrow strip between the water and the steep cliffs rising almost vertically out of the fjord. The cliffs were clad in bushes and small trees, grass and dandelions. In the spring she could find violets here. But the cliffs were dangerous. Every winter the wind and the rain and the waves crashed against them and sometimes caused slides that took trees and bushes and big parts of the cliffs down into the surf. They could be very wet and slippery. Father had strictly forbidden her ever to climb them.

Hannah was about to turn around and go back along the water's edge. She was completely absorbed in picking up little pieces of seaweed, sticks and shells to carry in her apron pocket.

Suddenly she froze in one horrifying moment of earsplitting terrifying roar. It was as if her skin contracted and a chill ran down her spine. Her ears were as if standing straight up in the air and her eyes widened up. She didn't move. Only her head turned in the direction of the noise. There, on the green to the west under the trees was a huge roaring monster, the same gray-green color as the soldiers occupying the country. The ones Father hated. Hannah knew immediately that there were soldiers inside even if she could not see them. They were starting up the engine of the monster which had long caterpillar strips where there normally would be wheels.

Then the incredibly long gun on it turned ever so slowly in her direction as it started to move out from under the thicket. It bobbed up and down a bit over the uneven ground as it slowly moved towards her, and the long gun pointed directly at the place where she stood. In a fraction of a second she knew she must flee. Her brain and her instinct woke up. The freeze lost its grip on her. She was completely alone on the beach. Her father and mother had no idea where she was or that she could be in danger from the soldiers. As quickly as the stickleback turned in the water, Hannah turned and flew like a gazelle towards the cliff. This was no time for obedience. The cliff was her only escape from the roaring monster that kept coming towards her. The monster would not be able to get up the cliff. She would.

She reached it in a few seconds and climbed like a squirrel, grasping whatever she could get hold of, forcing her feet into the wet clay and pulling herself up and up and up among the bushes and small trees, hoping that the soldiers would not be able to see where she was going, hiding behind bushes where she could, higher and higher till she reached the top about 200 feet above the water and on her stomach glided under the barbed wire that kept the grazing cattle from reaching the edge. Here she stood still to catch her breath and look down. The noise from the tank was still terrifying, but further away.

She leaned over the edge but could not see the monster. Her heart was pounding and she was out of breath after her climb. But not for long. She had to get home. She bolted across the pasture, in and out among the peacefully ruminating cows till she reached the road that ran between the inn and the town. She stopped and looked in all directions. She would hide in the grass if she saw anybody. She bolted across the road to the other side. Here was a neighboring farm and she jumped the hedge. Hidden by bushes and trees alongside the road she ran till she could see the inn and the barn.

But the noise from the tank seemed to be coming her way from the field. Gasping for air she flung herself down in the grass and listened. It was moving towards the inn. She scanned the road, it was clear between her and the barn.. She got up and again she flew like a gazelle across the road and reached the end of the barn just as the monster came up from the field heading her way. But she knew she was safe now, she flew past the barn and into the garden, round the house and to the front door of the inn. She came into the foyer panting just as Father was on his way to the dining room.

"Where have YOU been?" he asked.

Hannah told him – in staccato sentences – trying to get her breath back – about the tank and the soldiers hidden inside – coming towards her – and how she had outsmarted them – climbing the cliff and running home. She wanted Father to be proud of her.

His face turned dark. "Those rascals," he said, "they have nothing better to do than to scare little girls. They are here to be fattened up till they can be sent to the front to fight. I don't think they would have hurt you. But don't ever go alone so far from home again. This used to be your playground where you were safe. Now we have a war and it is going to get worse and more dangerous."

Hannah had not been afraid. That was a great satisfaction. She got away from the enemy. She still had her shells and pebbles in her little apron, and she walked proudly next to her father into the dining room.

∽

Just as Father had said, it was going to get worse and more dangerous. The following year more soldiers were stationed at the inn. Father had to give up one of the large halls. One day the children were told to stay indoors. When they protested, Anine, who had come from the village to help out, told them that their parents were very upset, because they had been told that today a large company of German soldiers would arrive and take over the biggest of the hotel halls. "We all have to stay indoors until we know what is going to happen." Anine said. "You don't want to run out and be accosted or run over when their tanks and their war vehicles come roaring. Come out in the kitchen with me. I will make your some hot cocoa." And while they sat drinking their cocoa the noise began. First the thunder from the tanks and lorries coming into the yard, then the commandos, the shouting and yelling. Out hopped soldiers in green uniforms, orders were yelled at them, things were unloaded and carried into the hall. The children looked out the windows and saw a big, fat man in uniform screaming furiously at some soldiers. They saw all kinds of equipment being unloaded. And all kinds of strange looking material were stacked outside in the yard. Their home was surrounded by soldiers and cars and lorries and constant noise. Then they heard singing and saw a unit march by, singing a German march song. The children did not leave the house at all that day. Ana heard one of the maids tell the others that Father had no intention of moving the ten beehives behind the large hall. If the bees annoyed the soldiers, so much the better.

The following days they noticed soldiers digging large holes in the ground. The grownups called them foxholes. There were foxholes along the beach and behind the barn. In some places there was barbed wire fence. And soldiers came into the restaurant and ordered food. Father had been told that if he did not open the restaurant to them a catering firm would take over and be established at the inn. Again he had to give in to the Wehrmacht or accept strangers who might be collaborators and dangerous.

The stench from the uniforms when a group of soldiers passed one on the road was disgusting. The rage and fury from the German Feldwebel ordering the young soldiers around was disturbing at first, then despicable. After a while the children looked at him with contempt.

Hannah still walked to and from school. As winter approached the wind was often so cold and strong that it brought tears to Hannah's eyes. On the way home she could look down over the meadow and the blue fjord. Sometimes the fjord was so dark blue it was almost black even if the sky was grey. Once a week a large steamer came through. Where did it go? Her imagination took her to places she had only read about in story books.

When alone on these long walks she talked to herself, was aware of herself as a person. When she was with the grownups she sometimes felt as if she was outside herself, always on guard when others wanted to decide over her. Sometimes she found a friend in one of the maids at the inn and then she had a marvelous time, giggling and singing and horsing around.

One day Father told Hannah that she had to change school. There had been no bad incidents between the soldiers and the people in the village. The soldiers were very disciplined and under strict commands. But Father no longer felt it was safe to have her walk to school when there were soldiers on the roads. Also the weather was very cold.

Now she had to take the bus together with Bodil. It was tedious. Gasoline was rationed and there was none for private cars. The school bus had a big black stove on the back. The Driver had to stop once in a while and put some kind of fuel in it. It took an hour, sometimes longer to drive the 11 miles to school. She missed the private teacher she and Bodil first had. Now Meili had married and she and her husband were driving their car by putting a horse in front and having the reins come out through the front screen. That looked funny, but worked well. Especially it was nice when it was raining, Meili told Father one day when she came visiting. Father's car had been put on chocks. That was what most car owners did in the hope that they would be able to use their cars again in the not too distant future.

Hannah did not like her new school. She was shy to begin with, and being put into a classroom with almost 30 other children who knew each other was just horrible. There were very annoying boys who used swear words and were disruptive in class and made some teachers mad. Sometimes a teacher would slap a boy hard on the cheek, or grab the hair above his ear and pull up and up till the boy moaned in pain. Some of the teachers were not very nice either. And how was she going to make friends with anybody when she lived so far away. She had to go home on the bus every day!

Mother wanted Bodil and Hannah to learn to play the piano. They started at the same time. Hannah loved it and her teacher was mostly pleased with her. Soon she played better than Bodil, who was more of a bookworm and more interested in Math. Their teacher would sometimes praise Hannah and once said she was a wonderful pupil, and at one time she would scold her when she had not practiced enough. Noone had ever called Hannah wonderful, so from then on she really made an effort to do well.

One day Father came and presented the girls with an "Ausweiss" each. The Germans had put barbed wire all around the whole hotel compound, and there were now guards at several entrances.

"You have to show your ID cards every time you come and go," Father said, "so do not lose them. Keep them in your satchels at all times."

So the girls dutifully showed their IDs every morning before catching the school bus and every time they came back in the afternoon. But one morning they were late, or the bus was early. Coming round the corner of the carriage house they saw the bus waiting, slowly starting up.

Bodil sprinted and Hannah followed. The bus driver saw them and stopped to wait for them. Bodil ignored the German guard and ran past him without stopping. Hannah followed her. The guard called after her to stop and moved towards the middle of the road as if to stop her. But Hannah had no intention of being left behind and ducked around him.

"Halt, muss Ich schissen?" he shouted again, and took the gun off his shoulder in a threatening gesture.

"Go ahead!" Hannah shouted back as she disappeared behind the bus and entered through the door. The bus took off. Hannah slumped down on the available seat next to Bodil.

"Those stupid Germans," Bodil said, "you know – she was still gasping for breath - "that guard has been there every morning the last week. He knows who we are. He just wants to see our 'Ausweiss" because he is bored and wants to see if he can make us talk. I am going to tell Father."

Hannah's nose went up in the air. She felt important next to Bodil. Important and safe. "I did not stop when he shouted at me." she said with great satisfaction.

That afternoon when they came home Bodil complained to Father: "Those stupid guards, they see us every morning and afternoon. Why do we have to stop every time to show our IDs? They know us by now. The guard this morning shouted after us although he knows we have to catch the bus. We just ran past him."

"Don't ever do that again," Father was serious, "some of them are desperate. They know they may be sent to the front and get killed. They have to obey orders. They could get away with shooting at you. You have to stop and show your I.D. Every time! I will rather have you miss the bus than get shot."

Bodil and Hannah exchanged glances, obviously thinking the same thing. "Why would anybody shoot us?" asked Bodil, "We were just running to catch the school bus. Any guard could see that. Are they stupid?"

"No," said Father, "but they can get away with almost anything. That is why we have to be careful. Do not make them angry. They have their orders and they have to obey their orders."

Father had been in the Danish army when he was young. He knew about rank and tried to make his girls understand.

But it was not easy for the girls to know how to behave always. A couple of days ago the big, fat, obnoxious German Feldwebel had come barging into the kitchen while they sat there. He was the one who always marched the young recruits up and down the road, bellowing out words in German and sounding very intimidating. When he had come into the kitchen he had shouted at Father in German and banged his fist on the counter. Only Father was not afraid of him. Father got out of his chair, quite red in the face. The girls could see he was angry. They sat very still.

"In this house I am the boss," Father had said in a loud voice as he stood a couple of inches taller than the Feldwebel, "and I will not have you or anybody else go into my private loft where you have no business. And if it happens again I shall immediately report you to the Commandant! Is that understood?"

With a sheepish look on his face the Feldwebel had clicked his heels and turned around and left the kitchen. The girls had watched in silence. Father could complain to the Commandant, the Feldwebel's superior. So why could they not complain to Father!

Bodil and Hannah finished their tea. They lived among enemy soldiers while a horrible war raged around them. But they always felt safe with Father, no matter what. They just had to learn certain rules. They would do as he said.

Mother wanted her girls to wear skirts or dresses, but the winters during World War II got very cold, so cold that the seamstress who often worked for Mother made them long woolly pants, and they were given sturdy leather boots. Some mornings Father would walk them to the bus, it was so cold he did not want them to go out in the dark and cold mornings alone.

One afternoon when they cam home from school they saw a soldier with a gun standing guard at the side of the carriage house. Then they saw he stood guard over somebody lying on the ground, covered with a blanket. They came into the big kitchen where the cook made tea for them. "We saw somebody on the ground where a soldier stood guard!" Bodil said.

The cook almost sputtered: "A young soldier shot himself. Why can't they shoot Hitler instead of sending them young boys to war? He had probably already lost his father and brother and uncles in the war and knew his turn to be killed was coming, so why not kill himself first! This war is ridiculous. Some of these boys must be straight out of High School, 15 and 16 years old. It is criminal. They should be home in school, where they belong. What is the world coming to?"

She poured the girls some tea brewed on cherry leaves and placed her homemade rolls with margarine and Rosehip marmelade in front of them.

Hannah had not thought of the soldiers as human beings who had families. They were just soldiers one did not even look at. The grown ups had said from the very beginning of the war: "Don't look them in the eyes, walk past them as if they do not exist!" Now the cook made her understand the young soldiers were victims too, victims of the war. That they had to obey orders or die.

On and on, day after day the soldiers marched and sang their songs: Songs like "Wir marchen gegen Engeland', 'Im Lande die Azoren'. 'Deutchland, Deutschland uber Alles'. And sometimes a whole company was sent away to fight somewhere, and a new company turned up.

During the third year of the war even children were sick and tired of the German occupation, because it affected them in many different ways. Part of their school was confiscated, first of all the big gym hall where they used to have so much fun. And the school bus was available to residents along its route because many people had no other way of getting to town. This meant the bus was usually so crowded that the children were forced to stand up, for they were expected to politely give up their seats to the grown ups. Some big homes had to rent out a room or two to German officers. On farms with big main houses sometimes several soldiers were stationed there. The war now affected everybody.

All over the country girls had enjoyed crocheting caps in red, white and blue, the same pattern as the round mark on the English spitfires that would fly over Denmark at night and drop ammunition to the freedom fighters. The sight of girls wearing the caps everywhere in the streets finally irritated the German Wehrmacht so much that they were outlawed. The boys loved to annoy the soldiers whenever possible. So at breaks when the children came outside the boys would sometimes do mock stretch march on their side of the barbed wire that ran down through the middle of the school yard, and sometimes they were heard shouting: "Best, Hitler, Himmler!" the names of infamous Germans. But pronounced that way in Danish it meant that the best Hitler could do was to fantasize about victory. The average German did not know that and nodded approvingly, to the infinite delight of the boys.

Ragnhild Munck

During the winter months life at the hotel was never as busy as in summer time. Often on winter evenings Mother would sit and repair clothes or knit while Father would read aloud for the whole family. They would gather in the sitting room. The windows were covered with the mandatory black curtains. From the stove came sputtering noises from the burning logs, and on top of it there was either a kettle with water, or on special occasions Father would place apples on it which they would eat with sirup or honey and cinnamon on top. Life seemed perfect and peaceful on those evenings. Mother was always careful that nothing be thrown away. A coat was turned inside out. Shirts were repaired by using the bottom part of it to create a new collar. Dresses and coats could be altered. Children would wear 'hand me downs', because it was difficult and expensive to buy good quality new clothes. One evening Mother asked Ana to thread a needle for her. Ana had perfect eyesight and did it easily and Mother thanked her and said how great it was that Hannah had such good eyesight. Hannah smiled with pride. Mother had praised her. She never forgot. It usually never happened. Often she was in the way and was scolded, so she would go to her room sobbing, wondering "Why does she not like me? Why does my Mother not like me?" So when once in a while she received praise she kept it alive in her heart.

When Hannah turned 11 years old, her godmother, Aunt Hannah, gave her a puppy, 9 weeks old. It was a wonderful gift, and she called him Chang. It was an expensive gift, a well bred brown and white pointer. Chang became her dearest friend. She kept him close, talked to him, ran with him, wanted him to be with her everywhere. But she had to go to school and leave him home. In the beginning it worked out well, but one day when he was about 7 months old, she came home and was told he had run after the mailman who came on his bicycle every morning to deliver mail. That could not be tolerated. So Hannah begged the maids and Mother not to let him out when she was at school. But somebody always let him out anyway and did not bother to get him back in.

One day Hannah and Chang were in the yard when the mailman came on his bicycle. Chang started barking and ran after him. The mailman wobbled on his bike and shouted that this dog should not be allowed out when it ran after cyclists. Hannah ran after Chang, grabbed him by the collar and hit him. What else could she do? That was what

Mother did when she found Hannah naughty. Chang tried to back away from her and then looked at her with scared and begging eyes.

Hannah started crying with remorse, "You do not hit somebody you love," a little voice said inside her, "it is wrong to hit anybody!" She lifted her dog up in her arms and carried him around to the garden. There she sat down and cried with her arms around her dog and told him she was sorry and that she would never hit him again. And that he must not run after people. For it would make the grownups angry, and then who knew what they might do. She found a string so she could hold him, when they were close to the road.

She was out of school for the summer holidays and the two of them ran along the beach and up in the hills. Hannah had a wonderful friend who loved her, followed her everywhere, never got tired of her, was her best friend. When summer vacation was over and she had to go back to school she begged everyone to keep Chang in, so he would not run after anybody, but Mother said they could not keep him indoors all day. He was let out again, and again he ran after cyclists. One day a farmer from beyond the village was talking to Father in the yard. He saw the dog and asked if Father used him when shooting, for otherwise it was a waste to have such a fine specimen around, and the farmer would surely like to have him. He could provide another puppy for Hannah, a German Shepherd she would love as much. When Hannah heard this she protested wildly. Noone should take her dog away from her. She ran out in the field with him, till they were both tired. She implored all not to let him out while she was at school, but every day when she came home, somebody had let him out anyway. And he had run after the mailman or somebody else. One day Mother said: "The dog has to go!"

Hannah hated the farmer for turning up. How could he even think of taking her dog away? It belonged to her. How could the grownups agree to it? She was heartbroken. She cried and protested to no avail. One day the farmer turned up with a little brown puppy that was put in a sty in the cowshed because Hannah refused to have anything to do with it. She did not want another dog. She would not hold it or have anything to do with it. She saw the farmer drive away with her dog. Chang sat and looked at her out of the car window as he was driven away. Ana ran away and cried.

Next day when she came home from school, one of the maids called out to her: "Hannah, your dog has come back!"

She was jubilant. Chang had found his way home. He stood in the yard with a broken string trailing after him. He belonged to Hannah. Surely the grown-ups could see that and not take him away again. He had run all the way home by himself to be with her.

Then suddenly the farmer was there, got out of his car and picked Chang up. "He has a good nose, that dog", he said, "I will have to take better care that he does not run back to you." and then he drove away with Chang again.

Hannah ran up in the hills and cried her eyes out again.

Two days later Chang was back in the yard. This time Hannah did not wait a second. "Come Chang," she shouted and ran as fast as she could towards the woods. She was not going to wait for the farmer to turn up again to take him away from her. She sat with Chang in her arms and told him how much she loved him and that she hated the grownups for taking him away from her and that she wanted him always to run home to her if they took him again. She did not go home till it grew dark.

Mother was angry that she had stayed away so long. The farmer had been there to pick up Chang who was nowhere to be found. Except they knew Hannah had him. It was wrong of her to run away with him they said.

But Chang was taken away and ran home five or six times. Finally one day Father said to her that this time she should get on her bicycle and take Chang back to the farmer herself. Father was gentle but firm. She had been given a new little puppy instead. A deal had been made. But Hannah never looked at the new puppy.

It was a trip she never forgot because she felt she was asked by her beloved Father to do something no little girl should ever have to do. It was her best and only friend and she had to take him away to a man she hated. She cried all the way and she told Chang she would always love him and that she hated the grownups. The farmer was in the yard when she got there and she did not even look at him, just handed Chang over and turned back.

That was one way to crucify a child

Her loyalty could not be bought. She never went to see the new puppy. She had not wanted it. It was not her puppy.

One day she was told the new puppy had died. Bodil and Mother blamed her: "You should have taken better care of it. It was your fault that it died. You never took it out."

That was the last straw. Finally her sorrow turned to rage. She screamed at them: "It was never my dog. Chang was my dog. They took Chang away from me. I did not want another dog. They took my dog away from me."

As she ran away crying she heard Father say that nobody should blame her. It was bad enough that she had lost the dog she loved. Somehow he understood, only this time too late for her and Chang.

Aunt Hannah came on a visit again. She was not happy that the dog had been given away, but she was a guest and did only comment on it once. She brought with her a small fine toothed comb and announced that the war had reintroduced lice in the population. In the schools all children had to be checked for lice. So she checked the children for lice and luckily found none.

Everything was getting more and more difficult. Soon people only had peat to use in the stoves. No wood or coal. Everything was rationed. Real coffee had not been available since the war broke out, and the substitutes were hardly worth drinking.

Father had kept some coffee beans for special occasions. He also had kept cocoa, and the children every week were given a spoonful of cocoa, some sugar and all the oats they wanted. They would mix it with a little butter or milk and make small cocoa balls and eat this instead of the chocolate no longer to be had. Kai would use so many oats it was hard to believe he could even taste the cocoa. Hannah thought his portion looked like brown porridge, but for Kai quantity was more important than quality. The grownups could not get decent tobacco, and some people started growing tobacco for home consumption. Father was happy to have his Jersey cows. They produced such wonderful fat milk that Mother could make her own butter, even icecream on special occasions.

Farmers had to report to authorities how many pigs they had and produced. Some were able to hide one or two for private consumption. Some tried to buy or sell on 'the black market'.

It was no longer possible to drive out to the North Sea Coast from where Father used to get lobsters and all kinds of seafood The Germans were building bunkers all the way from the border to the top of Jutland. Allegedly to stave off an English invasion, an idea Father said was ridiculous. Some villages had been evacuated completely. Families had to move. These were scary times with insecurity, lack of many goods and products taken for granted before the war. The grownups complained about it, but it became the norm for the children. They grew up used to seeing enemy soldiers everywhere, knowing they had to be careful about what they said and did.

One day at school one of the boys in Hannah's class brought in leaflets and placed one on each table. "Take them home," he said," but don't tell where you found them. Just give them to your parents." Hannah stuck one in her satchel and gave it to Father when she got home. Father took it and looked it over. "Be careful, Hannah," he said, "if the Germans discovered you carry this around they would start asking you questions. We would not want that. I would rather you did not touch it. Here we live in a hornets' nest. It is dangerous."

Hannah understood. She had seen how the boys sometimes tortured each other in the school yard, and how they purported that the Gestapo did this to the saboteurs they caught. It was scary and horrible. There were all kinds of rumors about people who disappeared and went 'underground', because they were hunted by Gestapo, the most feared Germans. The boys in schools talked about women who went out with German soldiers. They were called whores or 'German mattresses'. There were dangers everywhere. It was a matter of course that one was always aware of one's surroundings.

Ever more troops were stationed at the inn. Soldiers would be everywhere, visit restaurants and shops, sing their songs, go to theaters, behave if they owned the land. Some of them even thought they were welcome, may have been told that they were wanted by the Danes to make sure the English did not take over. At the same time sabotage became more and more frequent. Some factories would be blown up if they were producing materials for the German Wehrmacht. Railways were bombed to hinder German transports. Who was a friend and who was an enemy? There were Danish men and women who were informers. And freedom fighters who would kill them. It was an evil time when you did not know whom to trust. Father always had to worry about the hotel and the farm attached to it and people coming and going. Mother became more and more anxious.

Sometimes Hannah cried and cried when Mother had been after her. She would hide in her room and sob into her pillow and wonder why this was. Bodil was never chased around like Hannah was. Bodil was allowed to sit and read all the time, because she had always been frail Kai was a boy and should not do the same things as girls, Mother said. And Constance was still a little girl. Hannah would sometime dream herself away, wondering if she was a stepchild, wondering if she had a real mother somewhere else who some day would praise her and be nice to her. One day she read in a romantic book belonging to one of the maids the sentence: "she yearned for love!" That was like a revelation! 'That is what is wrong with me', she thought. 'I yearn for love. Why does my Mother not love me?' She started fantasizing. She had two godmothers, Aunt Hannah fairly close and Aunt Katrine in Copenhagen. Aunt Katrine she never saw but she sent wonderful presents for her birthday and at Christmas. Could it be that godmother Katrine who never married was her real mother and had given her away? She would go to sleep with that happy thought.

One day a girl called Oda, who got on the school bus outside her home, a grocery store a couple of miles past the inn, came and sat down next to Hannah and asked which grade she was in. Oda was almost three years older than Hannah, so they attended different classes. Oda had smart clothes and was very talkative, knew the bus driver and talked with him as if she was a grownup. She heard Hannah was from the inn and asked if they could sometime get together after school. They had bicycles and could visit each other in their homes. Hannah was evasive, said that they did not have much room left to themselves at the inn and that she was busy after school practicing the piano if not doing homework. Oda was not put off. One day she just turned up at the inn, came into the kitchen and said Hello and told Mother that she and Hannah went to school together and it was nice to have a friend in Hannah. Mother looked her over and asked who her parents were. She was offered a cup of tea in the kitchen with everybody else, and then Mother suggested she best go back home before it got dark, especially if she did not have a light on her bicycle.

"Can Hannah come home with me and stay overnight. Then we can take the bus together tomorrow morning. Wouldn't that be fun, Hannah?"

"No, Hannah has duties here at home. And it is 4.30. You need to leave now before it gets dark!"

When Oda had left, Mother said they did not know Oda's parents, but knew they were not churchgoers. She would not encourage their friendship.

Still it was the beginning of a long 'friendship', except Oda never was a true friend. She exploited Hannah's naivety to the utmost. Hannah was pretty. Oda was not. When aumt Hannah met her one day she commented afterwards: "She must be the least attractive girl I have ever set eyes on. She is ugly." Oda was also clever and manipulative and dishonest.

What Oda missed in good looks she had in abundance in boldness, smart clothes and candy. She could manipulate Hannah, who was brought up to obey, and to the sentence: 'the wiser child gives in'. Whenever there was an argument among the children Mother and Aunt Hannah always said: "The wiser one will give in." They wanted peace at any price.

Oda saw how the boys looked at Hannah, who was tall for her age and would soon grow into a pretty teenager. She also saw how many interesting and important people came to the inn, and that Hannah had important and well educated people in her family. Oda's father was the local grocer who also had a timber business and was fairly wealthy. But none in her family had a higher education.

Mother's instinct about Oda was correct. She did not think she was good company for Hannah and did not encourage it. But one day when Mother complained to a friend about Oda, the friend told her it was important that children had friends. So Mother let it be. Once in a while when Oda invited Hannah to stay overnight. Hannah did not have the guts to say No Thank you, if she did not want to, could not think of an excuse when Oda implored her, so she might give in.

Mother who was with child again became more impatient and short tempered:

"Do as you are told!" "Your will is in Father's pocket." "Because I say so!" You have to learn obedience!" "Who do you think you are?" "Don't answer back. How dare you be rude!"

Hannah could not remember she had ever sat on Mother's lab like the younger ones. They never touched. She never got a hug. But she often was told: "Behave yourself, Think about how much we do for you!" "Don't be so selfish!"

One day at school she heard Susanne and Oda say that their mothers were their best friends. Hannah could not believe her ears. How could that be? "My mother is a witch," she blurted out, "I hate my mother. When I was little she would put me in a little dark room and forget about me. And she would box my ears or pinch me when she got mad!"

There, she had said it. She was surprised at her own outburst.

One day in May when Aunt Hannah came to visit it seemed like spring had arrived. The sun finally came out and it was warm enough to have breakfast in the garden. It was wonderful after a long, cold winter. A white table cloth was placed over the table and fresh buns and wonderful butter and soft boiled eggs and homemade Rosehip marmelade was brought out with the coffee. "Oh, how lovely," said Aunt Hannah, "we are so lucky to have each other. And you are my special girl," she smiled at Hannah, "I carried you when you were baptized in the name of the Father, the Son and the Holy Spirit," and suddenly Aunt Hannah looked serious and sad and continued:"

"Then your Nana was also here. She loved all of you. And she thought you were very gifted and a gorgeous child. But it is a good thing she will not see the country occupied by the enemy"

Father came out with the newspaper in hand and sat down: "Good Morning, Hannah, how did you sleep! Did you ever get your chest of drawer back from Greenland?"

"Thomas, don't start teasing Hannah so early in the morning!" Mother said with an overbearing smile.

"Why does Father ask you about that?" Hannah looked at Aunt Hannah.

"Oh, he just likes teasing me," she answered.," when I was younger I thought I might spend some time as a nurse in Greenland. It just never came about, because the doctor who had suggested I joined him there canceled the whole thing. Now tell me, have you started swimming or is the fjord still too cold?"

"Of course we have started. We are vikings. I am up every morning a six!" Mother said.

"And how many soldiers have you got stationed here now? And do they behave themselves?" Aunt Hannah continued while eating a bun with obvious delight.

"Not so loud Hannah," said Mother, "there are many things we do not talk about."

But Father ignored her and said: "There are more than a hundred soldiers. And I am afraid more will come. They have our two large halls now, and they have to do what their officers tell them. If they do not behave I can complain about them to their superiors. But it is bad for business. We cannot have out usual big groups of people staying. My car I cannot drive for lack of gasoline. And if I had not bought several large bags of coffee beans we would not sit here drinking real coffee."

"But we are happy we have each other," Mother's voice was sad, "we hear about people who disappear."

"What news from the family on Zealand?" asked Father. Hannah had a feeling he did not want to be serious and sad.

"Oh, nothing new about Helge and Edith. I don't know how he can stand it. It is a tragedy."

"Hannah, not while the children are here, please!"

"Oh, I am so sorry, I did not know they are not supposed to hear."

Bodil had come out while she was talking. "Good Morning, my Dear, did you just wake up?"

"No", Bodil answered," I was reading a book!"

"Bodil has a good head. We hope she will go on to study when she grows up." Mother commented.

Hannah wished Mother would also say something nice about her, but she did not.

Every midsummer, when the sunlight stayed late in the evening and came back between 3 and 4 in the morning, it had been the custom to have celebrations on the huge, green field next to the inn. On Midsummer's Eve bonfires were lit everywhere and especially along the coasts in Denmark. People would gather around the bonfires and sing and dance, perhaps eat and drink. The custom was that a scarecrow in the shape of a witch would be on top of the bonfire. When the fire was lit, she was burned up. The legend is that she is being sent back to Bloksbjerg, a mountain in Germany, from where she comes.

Oda pleaded with Hannah's mother to be allowed to stay at the inn overnight. Mother said NO. She also said that Hannah was not allowed to participate, that she was far too young to be out late and join the games. And Mother did not approve of the gathering anyway. She felt there were too many temptations for young women who came and danced the night away. Oda pointed out that her parents allowed her to go, she would be with other young people from the village. Mother said 'no way', it was out of the question, and she sent Hannah to bed early. Hannah was furious, but had to obey.

A little after 10 o'clock there was a knock on the Hannah's bedroom window. She was there alone. When Hannah looked out, there was Oda, whispering: "Why don't you come with us?"

Hannah did not think twice. She dressed quickly and jumped out the window. It was not even quite dark outside yet. There was no wind and the fjord was like a mirror. Out over the water hang the moon and flooded the landscape. The evening was magical in its beauty. She could hear the singing from the green as they walked towards it. When they reached the green, the crowds were playing 'Blind Man's Buff', and there was a lot of laughter as the youngsters tried to catch each other. They continued with old and beloved songs and games, and Oda and her friends slipped into the ranks while Hannah stayed at the water's edge and watched.

'Why did mother not allow her to come here. It had always been her home, her playground, her fjord. There was no danger here, just young people enjoying a perfect evening'.

Watching the bonfire that was almost burned down, she dipped her hand in the fjord and licked her fingers, it was nice and salty. She sat down on a large rock on the beach. The moon rose higher and higher in the sky. Towards the East far out she could see no land. There was infinity, the unknown. And behind her the singing, dancing crowd as a moving human wave below the hills. She could hardly make out the long, low buildings of the inn at the end of the green. There were life's difficulties: a demanding Mother. There was also her Father, but he was so busy, it was almost as if he was not part of her life during the summer months. She did not have a single person she could call a good friend, not a single human being she felt she could trust and confide in, share everything with. The cook and the maids were her best friends, but they usually only stayed one year at a time before they disappeared out of her life.

While she sat there alone in the light of the moon, with the happy dancing crowd behind her, she saw the world was beautiful and filled with promises. The daily worries died away. There must be something great and beautiful out there in the universe.

In the pale moonlight under the gorgeous sky with the thousands of stars slowly coming into view on the pale firmament she stayed and listened to the happy singing behind her. She felt happy and calm, sitting there alone. Yet she did not feel alone.

As it grew darker the singing and playing stopped and groups of people started moving away. Hannah got up and walked along the water's edge without looking for Oda. She felt happy for having enjoyed this beautiful evening under God's magnificent heaven. She went back to her window and crawled back inside.

She had not been under her covers for two minutes before Mother was at the door.

"Where have you been? Father is out looking for you! How dare you go out when you have been told to go to bed!"

What could she answer. Suddenly she felt tired. The whole wonderful atmosphere was as if blown away. Why on earth had Mother checked on her after she had gone to bed?

"Do you want me to go and find Father? It won't take me long to run out and find him!" Hannah sounded defiant, not at all remorseful.

"You stay in your bed. Too bad we cannot trust you. How can you give your Father such grief!"

Reproaches rained over her, till Mother had spent herself. Then she closed the door firmly and left Hannah in her ruined mood.

If only Hannah could have answered back. But she had experienced too much abuse to answer back. When one is small, one is powerless against a grownup. It easily becomes a habit. One does not know if one will be subject to abuse, bodily or mentally, if one answers back. It is safer to keep one's mouth shut. And wait. Some day one will be grownup. Then one will remember how it was.

But when anger is not allowed to surface, for such is the pattern, then powerlessness takes over and turns into weeping. And Hannah cried. The beautiful evening ended in ugliness. She had sat there at the edge of her bed and looked at Mother raving. She had looked at Mother as if she was a woman who no longer meant anything to her. Only a year ago Hannah had said to herself in an hour of sorrow. "I suffer for unhappy love to my Mother. But nobody has any time for me. My Mother should give me love, but she only scolds me."

Now her longing for love had been pushed in the background. Now she was an observer who calmly looked at her Mother. And she saw an elderly woman who stood there with a distorted mouth and made herself ugly by ranting and raving.

It dawned on Hannah that there was no love between them. They were like strangers. There were no kisses and hugs between the two of them. If they ever touched it was when Mother slapped her or pinched her arms. And suddenly Hannah knew that this would never happen again. She had grown taller than Mother. No one should ever be allowed to hit her again. Bitter and angry she finally went to sleep.

When she met Oda in the school bus again, Oda asked how she had gotten home. Hannah told her that her Mother had found out and had been furious.

"My mother is never mad at me," said Oda, "my mother is the best thing in my life. I don't know what I would do without her."

Hannah just looked at her: "Really," she asked, "are there really mothers who never get mad at their children? My Mother is a witch."

She had said it again. Her emotions got words. It was no longer taboo to speak her feelings. She could break the silence. It actually helped. Part of the yoke was lifted. It had been said.

That day Hannah came home from school with a new sense of independence. Bad things in her life caused her to think more. It created distance. She quietly observed things and people. She was often engaged in her own thoughts when she was told to listen.

Mother's new pregnancy was an extra burden. She became more nervous and easily upset than usual and easily angry if any German soldier trespassed where they had no business to be. One Sunday afternoon Mother asked Hannah to come with her and help her make tea. When they came into the kitchen a pot stood on the stove with something steaming up from it.

"How strange," said Mother, "who is heating up coffee at this hour?" And she took the pot and poured the contents into the huge coffee machine that could hold 50 cups of coffee.

At that same moment the door from the foyer into the kitchen opened up and a German Feldwebel appeared. Mother turned around and spoke loudly: "Leave at once. You have no business in our kitchen. Close the door!"

The German Feldwebel stood like a statue for a second. He had seen Mother empty the pot and had understood her. His eyes narrowed to two splits in his red face.

"Sind Sie verrückt? Das war Glühwein." he shouted and he pulled out his revolver and lifted it so it pointed directly at Mother.

"Hier bestimme Ich. Wie wagen Sie das zu tun!"

Hannah instinctively moved two steps so she stood between Mother and the Feldwebel.

"Don't say anything, Mother, he could shoot you!"

Hannah had no sense of danger to herself. She could hardly remember not seeing soldiers around her home. They seemed no more dangerous than the boys in the schoolyard. She and her siblings had never been accosted or had reason to be afraid. But she felt instinctively that this guy could actually get away with shooting her mother.

At that moment another man in uniform with a white scarf around his neck appeared next to the Feldwebel and with a few words pushed him aside. Then he looked at Mother and said:

"Verzeien Sie Gnädige Frau, und Bitte – passen Sie auf. Wir wünchen keine Undglücksfälle. Und die Krieg wird ja schon zu Ende sein!"....or something to that effect. Hannah tried to repeat exactly what was said when Father turned up.

Father was quite upset when he heard about the episode. Mother tried to downplay the situation, but Hannah mentioned every detail:

"He could have shot Mother. You know the fat Feldwebel who always shouts at the soldiers. He is so obnoxious and horrible. He was so mad because his red wine was ruined."

Father knew and told Mother her temper might still get her killed and leave her children without a mother and him without a wife. They were lucky that the petty officer with the scarf had turned up. He was decent and hated the war as much as the Danes did. Which he demonstrated by wearing his white scarf, against all regulations.

Mother said that she had no way of knowing that there was red wine in the pot and the Germans had no business coming into her kitchen. She had to assert herself.

That evening after supper Hannah suddenly heard Father's angry voice in the foyer. She went into the kitchen where Mother sat on a chair, visibly shaken.

"What is happening?" she asked.

"Don't go out there," said Mother, "let Father take care of it."

"But what happened?" Hannah asked again.

"Somebody dropped a bag of sand from the second floor. It would have hit me if Father had not arrived just then. He came like an angel."

There were still loud voices in the foyer. Hannah had rarely heard Father so angry. After a little while he joined them in the kitchen.

"They would have killed you," he said to Mother, "if I had not heard your yelling at them and had arrived soon enough to pull you away that bag of sand would have hit you. It weighted at least 200 pounds. It was dropped by that scoundrel Lillegaard, the Danish informer they have installed here. Too bad that we have to fear one of our own more than the Germans.

I just wanted to make sure the cook could get to her room without being accosted," said Mother, "after all she is our responsibility."

"She is old enough to take care of herself," said Father, "the sandbag hit the floor so hard that the bag burst and the sand is all over the foyer. We are lucky the officer in charge came along. He seems to be the only one who can keep these rascals in check."

It wasn't just scary, it was sickening that a collaborator had been installed at the inn. Now they all had to be even more careful about what they said, since he could understand them and report to the German authorities.

Hannah went back to her homework. It was just another day in her life.

Every night at a certain hour Father turned on the radio and sat with his ear very close to it. He wanted to hear the news from England, as the news from the Danish Radio were censored by the Germans. Father did not want anyone to find out he was listening to England. They lived in a house surrounded by Germans. Only the family knew and listened in. Ana wondered about the greetings at the end of the forecast. There were greetings to a number of people, males as well as females. "Who are these people?" she once asked Bodil.

Bodil seemed to know everything: "They are sending messages to resistance fighters. The English are dropping ammunition to the Danish saboteurs, so they can blow up trains and factories used by the Germans. I read the illegal papers we sometimes get at school."

∞

In the beginning of October 1943 there were all kinds of rumors. A boy, Joseph, did not come to class. One of the boys said that Joseph would not be back. The family had disappeared. They were Jewish. The Germans were looking for them. Ana was never aware that somebody in school was Jewish. She only heard about Jews in church or in the Bible, because Jesus was Jewish. When she told Father and Mother about Joseph they looked sad and anxious. Father said:

"They are Danish citizens, and now they are being haunted. We live in evil times. What is next? It is happening all over the country. It is hard to believe we have to watch decent human beings being haunted in our country which used to be so peaceful."

Aunt Hannah was visiting and told Father that she had a Jewish couple staying in her apartment till they could get away to Sweden. Hannah overheard her and asked how long they would be staying and how would they get to Sweden. First aunt Hannah was horrified that Hannah had heard, then she said: "Hannah, promise you will not mention this with a single word to anybody. It could mean their death. It is terrible what this war does to people. We all have to help the Jews. They hope to get across to Sweden, where they will be safe."

There were other horror stories. They heard about English planes

A Warchild   59

being shot down. Sometimes the pilot was killed, other times he was rescued and helped away. It was dangerous to pick up the ammunition that was dropped by them. Resistance fighters might be caught if the Germans got wind of it and got there first.

One of the books Father would read to the whole family on quiet evenings was written in 1942 by a priest and author called Kaj Munk. Father had bought one of the first 500 copies printed and one evening started reading the very first page where it said that in this book noone was being shot, not a sound from a machinegun was heard and that he really should apologies for writing the book now, as most memoirs were written when one was 80 years old. Partly because one no longer remembered very well at that age, partly because those who would get angry would be dead by then. So when he wrote his memoirs now anyway the reason was.." The blank space may be filled in later, dear readers."

It was a beautiful book. The title was: "Spring comes so very slowly..". Kaj Munk wrote about his childhood, how he had lost both his parents when he was a child and how his life had been till he had his first play accepted to be played at the Royal Theater.

So the children felt they knew Kaj Munk well. And aunt Hannah told them he had once slept in her apartment where her bedstand missed a round wooden ball on a poster. To compensate she had placed a big, red apple in its place. Kaj Munk had written a thank you note and said he could not resist eating the apple. So ever since then aunt Hannah would have a red apple sitting there.

All who wanted to join and listen would gather after supper in the sitting room if Father was reading. Among others they heard 'Oliver Twist', 'The Field Core Stories' and 'It is Cheaper by he Dozen'. Sometimes Father would start laughing and stop reading, and the children would shout: "Read aloud, read aloud!" Once he refused to keep reading. "We will skip this one!" he laughed. And no protest from the children could persuade him to go on. Later Hannah found a chance to look in the book. In the story the father in the book had asked one of his boys to stand in front of his car. Then his father pressed the horn so the poor boy flew in the air in surprise. But the boy later got revenge. One day when the father had his head under the hood to fix something the boy went and pressed the horn, and the father emerged with eyes wide open, exclaiming: "Jesus Christ!"

Hannah laughed. Of course Father could not read that aloud. Mother would have objected. You did not take the Lord's name in vain! Out of the question! That would be blasphemy! Sinful! "We are born sinful!" Mother sometimes said. Hannah thought that was nonsense. How could a baby be born sinful. She once said it aloud, which Mother did not approve of. Hannah had to learn humility and not think she was wiser than the theologians.

Father and Mother tried to avoid talking about death and torture when the children were around, but other grownups in the inn were not so careful. And there were always children at school who knew about bad things happening. When women from the village came to help at the inn they would mention girls who fraternized with German soldiers. That would not be forgotten after the war, they would forever be stigmatized, they said. They mentioned a saboteur in town who had been sent to Neuengamme, a concentration camp in Germany. His sister had a child with a German soldier. She was thrown out of her parents' house. They would have nothing to do with her and the child. If you collaborated with the Germans you were a traitor, branded forever. There were some who would run with the hare and hunt with the dogs, hoping to survive as Danes if the Germans lost the war or be important in Hitler's millennium if they won. Sometimes one did not know whom to trust. Father had emphasized this often and said it again when the Danish collaborator moved into the hotel. "Lillegaard is an informer, never talk to him." So they were warned.

One day most of the hotel rooms were taken over by the German army for their officers. Only the rooms where the maids slept were on a different loft and completely closed off. One of the maids was a 35 year old woman, who had been with them for several years. She was hard of hearing, a kind and faithful and rather naive helper, always in good spirits and hard working. Her name was Henriette. Other maids came, usually for a year at a time. But as the war continued and ever more soldiers were stationed at the inn, it became difficult to find good helpers who would want to work there. Father's brother, Christen, had two daughters who had always been welcomed guests and playmates for Bodil and Hannah during school vacations. The oldest, Maren, agreed to come and work at the inn after having finished her exams. Hannah was ecstatic when she heard it. Maren was three years older than Hannah, was full of fun, good looking and independent. Whenever she had come to visit she would ask Hannah to play the beloved American songs she had at the piano. 'Poor Old Joe', 'Carry me back to Old Virginia' and all the other favorites. Maren would open a window and bellow the songs out with all her might. "The soldiers irritate us with their marching songs, now we can irritate them back with American songs!" she would say.

∾

One day Oda came to visit and immediately asked: "Has your cousin arrived?"

At that same moment Maren came through the door: "She most certainly has. She arrived at the hotel greeted by a parade and gun salutes protesting her invasion, but she conquered as planned!"

And then Maren, wonderful Maren, slumped into a chair, laughing. Maren had beautiful breasts, which Hannah admired with wonder. Already the first day Maren was there, Mother had said that she ought to get a bra in order to 'keep all that together'. Hannah was indignant. Was Mother going to decide over Maren? Maren could not help what she looked like, and that she was so goodlooking. It was wrong to suggest there was anything wrong with her looks.

But Maren just shook her head with her golden hair, looked at Mother in surprise and said that she had never had such a thing and it was probably expensive and she did not want to spend her money on such a 'thingummy'. And she had burst into a very contagious grin. So Mother remarked that she was still growing and that at this hotel so many came and went, so it was not the place to exhibit too much. That Maren would soon turn 17 and at the hotel were many soldiers. "Perhaps Father and I can take you shopping in town some day."

Mother would have things her way, but when she hinted there was something wrong with the way Maren looked, Hannah became defensive on her behalf. She admired Maren. who had no qualms saying what she thought about things and who had such a wonderful laugh. Hannah considered Maren a grownup............ almost. She was used to Mother's comments to herself, but not to Maren. If Hannah laughed too loudly, Mother would say: "Calm down a bit. There is no reason to go off the rails. It is not suitable for a young lady. It is not that amusing!" But to admonish Maren! That in Hannah's mind was not right.

And here Maren came and was just herself and dared say what was on her mind and express surprise if Mother suggested she behaved in a different way. Since Maren was Father's niece, Mother appealed to Father and said that Maren was a country girl and primitive and needed to learn manners.

When Hannah was with Maren it was like having a party every day. She was full of energy and fun and loved to sing. "Lets go 'American'", she would suggest. One of Hannah's aunts had given her the 'American Negro Spirituals'. There was a photo of Paul Robeson on the front page, and Bodil said he was a famous singer. Hannah quickly learned to play all the songs. Maren would stand behind her and bellow out the tunes. Oh, what a happy time they had.

"Damp down a bit, you are too loud," Mother would say. And Hannah felt that everything had to be 'damped down' except Mother's own temper. Hannah's face could take on an ice cold demeanor. She could hardly be blamed for the way she looked so long as she did not stick out her tongue! She had learned to put on a face of 'standoffishness', so Mother could not read her soul and innermost thoughts.

The old aunts and uncles did not take Mother very seriously, especially not uncle Henry. Perhaps that was the reason Mother wanted obedience from her children. Uncle Henry once was heard saying: "Thoughts are private, Trude!" And Mother's friend Agnes came from Copenhagen as a breath of fresh air. She was dressed after the latest fashion, always had bright red lipstick and nails, swept through the house as if she owned it, told jokes and stories and was once heard shouting at Mother:

"That has got to be a whale of a lie!" to which Mother would say: "Agnes, please, not in front of the children!"

Ana loved the unrestrained hilarity that Agnes brought. Agnes would help wherever needed, swing the laundry basket together with Anine and hang clothes out to dry. She would tease the farmhand and fool about with the cook till they all crumbled up with laughter. If Agnes suggested that Mother use a little powder and rouge she was met with indignation.

"Vanity is not a virtue. Anybody who behaves well is pretty enough." When somebody paid her daughters a compliment, Mother would stop them: "Do not mention it when they are around. It is not good for them!" They were not to be praised or made a fuss over. But Mother's friends did and said what they wanted.

Mother wanted to control Maren, but she never succeeded. Maren helped willingly with chores and did her work well, but she had her own opinions and voiced them. She was not used to Mother's way of reign.

Hannah loved to come home from school now Maren was there. When she always had to catch the bus home she could not mix with friends in town.. At lunch hour she would sit and chat with others who like herself came in on a bus. But that was it.

Once they got a new teacher in German, a lady who was rather nervous and who could not keep the boys in check. Hannah listened in awe to the boys:

"It is one hell of a stupid language, which we will never use. When the war is over all the Germans will have been killed. And if a few have survived we will make sure they are haunted to death." or

"We are not interested in learning German. Why can't we have twice as many hours learning English instead?" or

"The only ones who need to speak German are the informers, and when the war is over we will hang them all."

One day the Principal came into the classroom and admonished the boys. He wanted order and discipline. No provocation on the playground. He wanted all the students to be aware of the fact that they lived in dangerous times. It was important for them and their parents that they behaved in a dignified way.

"Dignified way!" one of the boys snickered, when the Principal had left. "My mother's brother has been imprisoned by the Germans. I am sure they do not behave in a 'dignified' way towards him. Mother says they have tortured him. And those f...... informers are to blame."

When Bodil started at Aunt Ellen's boarding school, Mother did not say why, namely that Bodil was growing into a lovely teenager. Ana was as tall as Bodil but she was not a temptation to young men, had not developed breasts and a woman's body yet. Mother thought that one way of protecting her daughters was that they knew as little as possible about the dangers and temptations of the world.

Ana always wanted explanations. She wanted to know as much as possible. Sometimes she heard things at school about relationships between men and women, told by boys in a smutty way. That was embarrassing to listen to.

Bodil came home from boarding school for the Christmas holiday. Hannah looked at her with admiration. She had become an attractive young woman, almost a grownup to look at.

Father and Mother did everything they could to create a good Christmas in spite of the circumstances. A tree was decorated with old and treasured ornaments and with real candles. For dinner they had roast goose with red cabbage and potatoes and for dessert a wonderful Ris a la Mande, for Mother still had some rice left from before the war, kept just for Christmas dinner; and of course they had the most wonderful cream from their Jersey cows.

Aunt Hannah came and Father's sister Aunt Andrea. It was tradition that any unmarried aunt was invited on special occasions, and these two aunts were dear beloved guests. On the top shelf in the big bedroom Father still had treasures from before the war. There appeared small pieces of candy and chocolates to put in the little cornets on the Christmas tree. And after dinner the grownups enjoyed a cup of real coffee. Mother had grounded coffee beans. There were homemade cookies and red apples. And presents for all, mittens and scarfs and warm woolen socks, knitted from homespun wool from their sheep. And new books. It was a feast.

Maren and Hannah were invited to dinner at Oda's home during the Christmas holiday. And they were treated to a lovely meal, during which Oda's father asked what they were doing on New Years Eve, for they would be welcome to stay there overnight and to bring Kai. Father and Mother immediately gave their permission, for it was not possible to do much celebration at the inn, with hundreds of soldiers around. It would almost be a relief not to have too many children around.

As was the custom in most Danish homes, dinner on New Years Eve was boiled codfish with all kinds of wonderful things to go with it, boiled potatoes and horseradish and melted butter and creamed curly kale. And a Trifle for dessert. Oda's mother had decorated a fabulous looking dinner table with little cornets filled with candy at each settings, and funny paper hats and rattles for everybody. Oda's older brother was home. He was full of mischief, and Oda's father told funny stories and it was just a wonderful time with laughter and songs. After dinner Oda's father said that now it was time to go for a walk and see what young people were up to in the village. Out they went in the cold winter night. At one house they saw a gate that had been hoisted up to the top of a flagpole. Another place a blue coffeepot was dangling from a chimney. It was a night of mischief. Oda's father knew everybody in the village and talked and joked with all they met. After a while he said he would go back to his wife, who only walked with a cane, and he did not want to leave her alone for too long.

"Lets join the others," said Oda, and they followed a group of youngsters. At a fairly big house some of the boys kept throwing bangers into the foyer.

"Why do they keep throwing bangers into that house," asked Kai. They stood a distance away and watched.

"Because it is New Year's Eve and the man who lives there in not a nice man!" said Oda, "he does not like children and is always so grumpy. And he beats up anybody he can get hold of."

Suddenly the door opened and a man stormed out. The boys scattered to the winds and disappeared.

"Run", shouted Oda and took off. Maren and Hannah and Kai followed, but Kai was not fast enough. Suddenly Hannah heard him call her. She stopped and saw that the man had Kai by the arm and was dragging him into the house. She was horrified. What would the man do to Kai and how was she going to get him out of there.

"I am going back to knock on the door and get Kai out," she announced and turned around.

"Are you crazy, then he will also grab you. He will not let you go. We have to run home and get my Dad."

So they ran home to Oda's Dad and told what had happened. He immediately went to the phone and they heard him talk: "So you have called the police? Oh, you could not get through to any. No, of course not. Oh, the guards on duty. You want them to pick him up?"

Hannah listened with fear in her heart. She would get in trouble with Mother for this. Then she heard Oda's Dad say: "You will not get them to come and pick up a ten year old lad who was not part of the group who bothered you. He was only watching the others. No Hans. I will come and get him. I am already on my way!" and she saw him hang up.

"Come Hannah, we will get Kai out. The rest of you stay here."

Hannah's eyes were big as teacups when they entered the door to the house where Kai had been dragged in. There Kai sat on a chair and looked very serious. The man called Hans was still angry, but Oda's Dad calmed him down and soon they left the house.

That was by far the most exciting new Years Eve they had ever had, and once Kai recovered from the shock of being caught he was rather proud of himself. When they came home the next day he bragged about it and luckily Father was not upset: "It was lucky you had somebody to bail you out." he joked.

∽

A week later Father called everybody into the bedroom. "Come and sit down." said Mother in a very serious tone, "Father has something to tell you!"

The children sat down on the big bed, and Kai moved close to Hannah as if he was afraid. Hannah looked anxiously at Father who said:

"I want to tell you before you hear it from anybody else. We have been reading Kaj Munk's book. He has been found dead, shot through the head and thrown in a ditch far from his home. We read "Spring comes so very slowly.." Now he will never see another spring. We live in a terrible time. Imagine shooting a parson and then throw his body in a ditch and drive away."

"The whole country is mourning," said Mother, "it is so terrible. His wife and five children have to go through this awful loss. May God show mercy towards us."

It was such shocking news. Hard to believe. They had recently read his book. It was as if they knew him. They left the bedroom and went into the sitting room. They did not want to go outside. There were German soldiers marching by. They constantly heard someone shouting angry commands. The guards were all around. It was almost as if something bad was ahead, as if something else might happen. Would Mother and Father be safe?

One day at school Hannah listened to Oda and another girl talking about their parents. "My mother is my best friend", said Oda and the other girl echoed her. "Mine, too! I don't know what I would do without my mother, she is always on my side."

Sometimes when Mother had been after Hannah and scolded her, Hannah would disappear into her room and fling herself on her bed and cry. "Why does she not care about me?" she would sob into her pillow.

"I don't like my Mother!" Hannah blurted out. There! She had said it again. Somehow it made her feel better to have shared. "My Mother is always mad at me. I can do nothing right. She used to slap me."

Oda nodded: "That is true, your Mother is often angry. She does have a temper and gets mad very quickly. I am glad soldiers are not all around my home, my Dad would get mad every day, I am sure."

However, Oda loved to visit Hannah and often commented on a soldier, if he was goodlooking or tried to get a conversation going with her when she came and parked her bicycle against a tree or a wall.

"Don't talk to them," Hannah warned her one day when Oda and Hannah walked down to the beach, and a soldier said something to her.

"Oh, Hannah, don't be silly. They are just young boys. They are not Nazis, they probably hate the war as much as everybody else. I can say Hi, that does not mean I am going to talk to them."

"Don't say anything!' Hannah turned around and went back to the house. Oda came running after her, "I didn't say anything. For God's sake!"

∞

On her 13th birthday Hannah was taller than both Mother and Bodil. As a birthday present she had wanted a new pair of shoes, for the ones she got half a year ago were already too small. Mother had been annoyed when she complained that they already felt too small. Hannah felt guilty for growing so fast, but Maren laughed at her and said:

"Just be happy it is your feet and not your boobs growing, otherwise you would be given a bra like mine." Maren had been with Mother and Father in town to go shopping, and Mother made sure Maren got a bra.

More soldiers had arrived and the Wehrmacht announced that they wanted every single hotel room and planned to bring even more soldiers.

This meant that all hotel business would cease and only the restaurant would be available to the public. And who would come to eat at the restaurant when it practically was inside a German fortress. Father had long been afraid this would happen. He now started taking the bus to various towns to look at hotels for sale that would not be occupied by the Germans. He said that they no longer could stay here unless this outrageous war soon came to an end.

When Father was away Mother became even more nervous and irritable. Tut, the youngest, was still a baby and when Hannah came home from school she would often take care of her. She asked Mother if she could stay home from school now since it was decided they would move whenever Father could find another hotel. Mother said absolutely No.

"We do not know how soon Father can find a hotel that is still functioning as such, and although you then have to change school, you cannot just stop now. The law is the law." Hannah would have loved to stay home and help now that Maren was there.

"I wish I were as old as you!" she said to Maren who just grinned and said she would be happy to wait for her. Only three years. You can pickle me. Then I would lose weight and your Mother could save her money and not buy me any more bras."

Maren stood to attention so her two breasts stood out. "Next time I have to make a speech, there are two points I want to make."

Hannah laughed, she felt so carefree and happy in her company. Maren had to go to the village to pick up some grocery "I will go with you." Hannah said. It was a nice walk.

"You know", continued Maren, "noone is more patrotic than I am. I would love to join the resistance movement if I could find a group. But how can I do that when I live here. We don't want to have anything to do with the Germans, but it is impossible not to talk with them when I have to serve in the restaurant. I have to take their orders. You cannot work here and not talk with them. I don't want to be friendly with the Germans. There is nothing I could wish for more than this war was over and that they all went back to their own country. And you know what? the soldiers who are here also hate the war. They do not want to be here. Some of them say outright that they are not Nazists. They want to go home. They say it out loud. And you know the handsome petty officer who walks around with a white scarf over his uniform. It is totally not acceptable to wear a white scarf over the uniform. But that is his way of protesting the war. I wonder how he can get away with it. He says he hates the war. So it must be hell for them to be here. Only one thing is worse, they say, that they will be sent to fight at the Russian front."

'How weird!' Hannah thought, 'Maren could understand all they talked about in the restaurant. Hannah never came near it. And she hated the smell of uniforms. When a group of soldiers passed on bicycles or marched passed her she held fingers around her nose to avoid the smell. Some said the uniforms were treated against moth. But they smelled like mice or old cheese, when they passed in a group.

Maren continued and could make anything sound amusing: "At the last table I had to serve fried potatoes and eggs. A chair was missing when the Feldwebel wanted to join them, so I picked one up in the hall and placed it at the table. When the Feldwebel sat down on it, the hind legs collapsed and he flew backwards along the floor. Gosh, how I laughed and so did they all in the restaurant. The Feldwebel picked himself up and pointed a threatening finger at me and said that was sabotage. But because all the others laughed he was somewhat disarmed."

"But you know," Maren went on, "if your Father had refused to operate the restaurant, the Wehrmacht would have brought in a catering firm who probably would have been friends of the Wehrmacht, and that would have been worse. They would have taken over the kitchen. And then we would have them in what is now our private space. And they would serve alcohol, and there would be informers."

When they came back to the compound and were about to go through the entry, some little devil got into Maren. She ran up to the barbed wire fence and jumped, thinking she could make it over. What started being an elegant jump ended up with her having a torn behind, a ruined apron and four scratches on her left arm. Still that was not the worst part. Turning the corner came three of the customers from the restaurant, and both they and the guard on duty split with laughter at the sight.

Hannah, who at first stared at her in amazement, ran to help Maren up and then, when she saw Maren was not seriously hurt, started to laugh, too.

"Oh, how awful," groaned Maren, "if only those turds hadn't seen me. There is the guy with the white scarf. I hate him for laughing at me!"

It had become a nightmare for Father and Mother to run the hotel. Every couple of months a new unit of soldiers came to be fattened up before going back to war. Father said the recruits got younger and younger or older and older. Mother's nerves were raw. She yelled if any of them dared to come into the kitchen and when they went into the foyer with dirty boots. Some totally ignored her, others yelled back at her. When Father heard her he always came to calm her down.

"You will only make them more nervous than they already are. They know perfectly well that they are not welcome here. For that matter they would rather be home in their own country. But we have a war raging, and they can be so nervous that they will take it out on us. We have to stay calm. They have tried to kill you once already. We cannot risk that happening again."

And then it happened that Father discovered that someone had broken into the private loft and stolen the inn's extra linen and pillows and comforters and his old blue uniform from way back when he had been in the Danish army. It was just after supper. Father came roaring down the stairs and into the restaurant where the Feldwebel sat. Father shouted so loudly that it was heard all over the inn. Everyone went silent. Noone had ever heard Father so angry. He kept on thundering. And then Father and the Feldwebel came out in the kitchen while Father was still shouting, furious and red in his face. The Feldwebel kept nodding and repeating: "Ja, ja, wir wollen alles tun...and a lot more which Hannah did not understand.

When Father had stopped speaking and the Feldwebel had gone back to the restaurant, Father went into the sitting room. And only then did Hannah and the cook and the maids look at each other and start talking again.

"Wow, your Father certainly knows how to gain their respect," the cook said, "when he really gets angry it is best to disappear. There was not a single German answering back. He is still master in his own house."

The cook was happy to bring a nice piece of gossip back to the village that evening. And yet, they all knew that the Patron had to put up with housing the soldiers just as all others with large houses. But it was really neat when somebody managed to give them an earful.

Maren had a diary. And she wrote poetry. One day she let Hannah look into it. She was totally amazed. How could anybody just write verses like this. But then she continued reading and there was something about a 'scarf" she could not make head or tales of.

"What on earth is that about?" she asked

At first Maren did not want to talk about it. Then she had Hannah swear silence for eternity if she did tell.

"You know the tall, handsome petty officer who walks around with a white scarf over his uniform?"

"Yes", answered Hannah reluctantly," That was the officer who turned up and saved Mother when the Feldwebel pointed his gun at her.

"He is every bit as handsome as Gary Cooper!"

At first Hannah said nothing. Was Maren just as interested in boys as was Oda? She suddenly felt childish. She was younger than Maren and Oda and far to shy to talk to boys. As a matter of fact she had never talked to a boy, more than perhaps five sentences, except to Kai, of course. She was hopelessly behind other girls.

"Who is Gary Cooper?" she asked

Maren just grinned: "Gosh, you don't know anything. Your Mother has never let you go to the cinema to see a movie, so I guess you cannot help it. He is the most stunning actor in America. And the 'Scarf' is just as handsome. I call him the 'Scarf' because he always wears that long white scarf. It is against all regulations, and I rather like that. He is not a Nazist. He is demonstrating that wherever he goes. It is a blooming shame he is German."

Hannah said nothing. This was odd. She did not even want to ask if Maren ever talked to him. Imagine, writing about him in her diary.

One day there was a cattle show on the green, one of the few functions that could still be managed by the hotel. There was a good show of cattle and many people turned up.

Maren complained that evening: "I have been washing dishes all day apart for a trip to fetch more milk and butter at the grocer. When I returned, the 'Scarf' and the senior Feldwebel were admiring a bull. As I walked past them the Feldwebel pointed at the bull and asked me: "Your brother?"

Of course I ignored him. But the bull took revenge on my behalf. It moved slightly, which caused the Feldwebel to take a couple of steps backwards to get out of its way. He stepped right up in a fresh cow pat. You should have seen his face. It was heavenly. I laughed so my cheeks and thighs were equally wet. Enough to make my belly hurt. Apart from washing a million dirty dishes it has been a hilarious day. After lunch I had an errand upstairs and on my way down, suddenly the 'Scarf' was there going up. We should have been able to pass each other, but he blocked the whole passage, so I stepped into the corner. Then he pricked me right in my stomach and made me retreat all the way up, thanked me heartily and grinning disappeared into his room. Later, he stuck his head out and asked if I was mad. I said yes and promised revenge. He offered me a big red apple if I would forgive him. I took the apple, but said I was not completely appeased. So now I will have to think of something.

Sometimes Hannah wondered how Maren could know so much. She had names for several of the soldiers.

"There is 'Stehenlassen', she said one day when she and Hannah had been to the grocer and passed a soldier on the way.

"Is that his name", Hannah asked in surprise.

"No, but he has a sign hanging on his bicycle saying that. I guess he is afraid one of the others will steal it."

Well, that was fairly obvious. Bicycles were for most people the only way they could get around. Hannah and Maren had bicycles with wooden rims. There was no rubber to be had. And most people were very careful with their bikes. She wondered how much Maren had to talk with the soldiers in the restaurant. Hannah was away at school from seven in the morning till four in the afternoon or longer if the bus was late. So a lot could happen at home while she was away. Even on Saturdays they did not get home from school till about three in the afternoon. Sunday was the only day in the week where it might be possible to sleep in, unless they had to go to church.

If the weather was nice they would walk to church across the meadow. That would be only 6 km. Otherwise it would be 8 km on bicycles that were ready to fall apart.

Hannah kept being amazed at how much Maren knew about everything, including the soldiers. Once on their way to the village they were struggling against the stiff west wind. Going the opposite way towards the fjord walked a tall soldier. His long, white scarf trailed after him in the wind.

"Halstuch, Halstuch", Maren shouted and waved as they passed him. Smiling, he waved back and shouted: "Alles gute, alles gute!"

"He believes you shouted 'Alles gute' to him, Maren. He cannot know you call him 'Halstuch'. Nor is it very nice."

Hannah felt embarrassed on behalf of Maren. She had stolen a glance at the man's face. He was the one Maren said was so handsome. She was right. He was goodlooking like Father.

"Ha, of course he knows that. How could that be a secret. I sometimes talk with him in the restaurant. His real name is Karl. He is a very nice man. It is a shame he is German. But of course he cannot help that. He has been fighting on the Eastern front and is only here for a while, then he will be sent back again, if the war goes on. He hates war."

"How strange," thought Hannah, "here in the village everything is so peaceful, even with a war going on and foreign soldiers around us. Here noone is shooting at them, no bombs are being dropped. But the soldiers who are hated by most people here can at any time be ordered out to fight and be killed. And if they don't follow orders they will be shot by their own. Here nobody is allowed to talk with them, have anything to do with them. And when they are ordered away, they most probably will be killed. How idiotic is war!"

"Are you allowed to talk to him?" Hannah asked. Her experience was never to say a word to a German unless it was something formal when passing the guards, or if someone came and asked to speak to Father. Her knowledge of German was not good, because she was not a good student, but at least she could understand most of daily talk.

"I cannot possibly avoid talking to them when I have to be waitress all day", answered Maren, "and I am so glad you bought me a notebook, so that I can write down all the things that go on. My diary shall contain my most precious memories and deepest secrets. It will be a comfort when I am sad, and it will make me laugh when I read something funny. And it will also make me realize the serious things in life. I have had this job for a relatively short time, but I have already experienced so much. I am going to write about you and Oda, Ruth and Henriette and the cook, and also about the 'Scarf" and the Curlyhead and the Obergefreideren, the small fat one, and all the other characters running around here."

They got home with eggs and onions. At least they had plenty of potatoes from the fields belonging to the inn. It was amazing amounts of potatoes and fried eggs that was served in the restaurant. The farm produced plenty of potatoes, but there were not enough chickens to provide all the eggs needed.

Father had always bought large amount of coffee beans, tea and sugar for the hotel, and when the war came and before everything was rationed he stocked up even further. Noone but he would ever go to the top shelf in the big closet in the bedroom, where it all was kept. Also soap became hard to buy, so Mother made their own from ox suet in the large copper in the scullery. And every week Henriette spent a whole day doing laundry, using a washboard in the large zinc tub.

But then one day the German military also seized the scullery and turned it into their kitchen when another large unit of soldiers came to the hotel. They brought their own large containers for cooking and their own cooks.

There were no more hotel guests. There was room only for the soldiers and the Danish informer who were installed there. He tried to get in touch with them by asking questions if they met, but Father had warned them ahead of time:

"Don't answer if he talks to you. He is an informer and far more dangerous than the soldiers. He will betray anybody. There are freedom fighters who are killed because of informers. Most of the German soldiers would rather go home and avoid being sent to the front, but informers are dangerous because they will report to the Wehrmacht anything they hear being said against the Germans."

One day in September 1944 news spread like a wildfire through the school: "They have taken the police! Sondergaard went underground, but they got constable Petersen. He will probably be sent to the Froslev camp. He could be shot."

The rumors circulated. The children were upset. They were used to seeing the police in the streets and knew them. They had all heard about the Froslev camp, a terrible place to be sent to and perhaps they would be transferred to even worse camps in Germany.

"Perhaps they will be tortured, and they do not get any proper food!"

Nobody knew exactly what a concentration camp was, only that it was a horrible place to be sent to. Worse than prison! Horror and fear of the unknown, and the rumors of starvation and torture were frightening. Their own police whom they knew and respected. Sondergaard and Petersen often walked on Main street and any boy being too fresh in their present would regret it. Now they had to go underground or be taken by Gestapo. Taken away. To a place worse than prison. The children knew that saboteurs got caught and were interrogated and tortured and sometimes shot. And now the constables, who always were there to help and keep order. It was terrible.

During breaks at school there were boys who wanted to show their contempt for the Germans who walked on the other side of the barbed wire in the schoolyard. But the teacher who had duty on the playground reacted immediately: "Get away from the wire, boys! You have no business here. Go to the other side. Off with you!"

When Hannah came home from school that day, Father talked to her and Kai: "Be very careful. We have no police now. The Germans and other scoundrels can get away with anything, and there is nothing we can do. If they notice people doing things they do not approve of, they can come and pick us up. People are being sent to places we only hear about, and nobody really knows what happens there. And nobody gets away from there. Be careful what you say. The Germans have Danish informers"

Then one day Father asked them all to come to the bedroom. "Come and sit down!" said Mother in a serious voice, "Father has something to tell us!"

Hannah and Kai sat down together on the bed. Kai got close to Hannah who looked with anxious eyes at Father. Last time they were called into the bedroom to be told something serious was when Father told them that Kaj Munk had been shot. That was after Father had read aloud his book "The Spring comes so very slowly". It was hard to believe he had been shot. And the newspaper had only been allowed to carry a small notice about it, which also made Father angry.

Now they were back in the bedroom, waiting to hear some other bad news.

"We will be moving soon," started Father, "to a hotel in Skorsor. We cannot stay here. 6 weeks from now I will take over the new hotel, and soon after we will have to be ready to move. You will of course have to change school. The hotel is in the center of town, and it will be a whole new situation to get used to. We all have to help each other. It is a very nice and newly built hotel, and there will not be any soldiers there. I have been told so by authorities. Every town must have two hotels available for travelers, and this is one of them. We hope that we can live there in peace and comfort till the war is over. Maren will move with us and later Henriette. But none of the other maids and not Kasper.

Kai started crying: "I don't want to move!" he snivelled.

Hannah said nothing, but she felt anxious. Kai was used to having things his way, so perhaps he thought it would help to cry. She had only once seen Kai being punished. That was when he had taken a big cigar out of the box Father used to offer guests from. He had tried to smoke it in his cave in the garden, but Mother had discovered it. He was put to bed and to shame, and everybody knew about it. But Kai was the only boy and therefore special and usually got away with more than the girls. And although Mother said that God loved all people and that she loved all her children equally, she probably did not know any better. It was obvious that her son was the most important. He was no longer a fat little boy, but a very sweet boy, and Hannah was protective of him if he needed help. Bodil liked teasing him, which Hannah could not stand. Once when Bodil kept teasing him they got into a fight and Bodil's long finger nails tore some long scratches in Hannah's face. Next day in school she was asked if a cat had made the scratches and she said Yes. She did not want anybody to know that it was her own sister who had done it.

And now they had to start in a new school again. She had to go into a new room full of unknown faces, boys and girls she did not know. It was unavoidable. Just as it was unavoidable for the soldiers to be sent to the front. One could be forced to do things whether one wanted to or not.

"What does it look like, Father?" asked Hannah, 'the hotel we are moving to?"

"There is a private apartment on the second floor in one end of the hotel, which is in Holme Street, "you may get your own room, we shall see. We have never lived in a town before, so it is going to be a big change. But we have to leave our home here, whether we like it or not. Mother and I are very unhappy about it. We have lived here for many years and been very happy. We have had a good business. But it is over. The soldiers will take everything. There will be two rooms left only, where aunt Hanna and Henriette will stay, as we are responsible for the phone exchange and for the premises, even though we no longer can use it as our business.

Father looked worn out and tired and unhappy. Mother sat with Tut on her lap and Constance close up against her.

"Stop crying!" she said to Kai, "it is no use. And remember it is going to be the King's birthday soon. Then we will have hot chocolate and Father says we will have a big cake to celebrate him. And grandfather is going to be here."

For a while Kai forgot the bad news for the good news. They went out into the kitchen. "Did you know we are going to move?" she asked Maren who was there.

"Yes, your Father told me already. I am so sorry. And I had just gotten used to living here. And I have gotten new friends. And did you know I was with your parents in town this morning. I got a lovely dress, shoes, underwear and stockings and a hat. I am overjoyed. Come up to my room and see."

Maren kept talking: "When we came back I had to go and help Kasper and Ruth to get some potatoes. I like working with them. And I took a swim afterwards. It was warmer than the air. And I ran soaking wet up the stairs to my room. It may be my last swim this year. I hate comments from the soldiers who may turn up anywhere at any time. But I am so sorry we have to move. I just love the fjord and this place."

Hannah stayed in the kitchen after supper and helped washing up. It was more fun being with Maren than anywhere else. Maren and one of the other maids starting singing "Oh, Susanna...' at the top of their voices, and Hannah and Ruth joined them while they dried and put plates and flatware away.

The window was open and suddenly they heard German soldiers applaud them from outside. At the same time Father came out in the kitchen and said. "You have to close the window and pull down the blackout curtain. Otherwise the soldiers won't get to bed tonight!"

They immediately stopped. They had not been able to pull down the blackout curtain in the serving room, it was in tatters. Would they ever get rid of these ugly curtains? They enjoyed singing the American songs and hopefully annoy the Germans with them. But they closed the window.

The next day the flagpole was taken down and a new rope was put in and the Danish flag was hoisted. That afternoon, September 26, they all came out on the lawn and sang 'King Christian', the Danish national anthem, and several other patriotic songs. Grandfather had arrived and said it was a good thing they still had their King in the country and now all Danes wished him a good birthday.

Then they were served hot chocolate and a big birthday cake with lots of whipping cream on. Maren had so much to eat that she suddenly declared she had to move. Kai and Constance ran after her, and then they saw her and the two children come marching around the flagpole each with a broom over their shoulder as if they were carrying a rifle, all the while bellowing out: "Dengang jeg drog af sted...", a beloved song written after a previous war with Germany. The words of the song started with: 'Once when I went off to war....'.

It was a sight to be seen. Hannah loved when Maren did something like that. It would never have occurred to Hannah to do it. But Maren did not care if she sometimes made fun of herself and had other people laugh at her. What a nice birthday party for the King.

That evening Maren and Hannah were invited to dinner at Oda's. They had soup and pancakes and did not have to be home till 9 p.m. The King of Denmark had stayed with his people, and they celebrated him.

Autumn came with cooler weather and a sense of finality. When Hannah came home from school Mother needed her to look after Tut and Constance or sort out things that had to be packed and ready for the big move. She hardly had time to do homework, nor practice on the piano. She did not care, she had to move to a different place, a new school and start all over with new people. The only fun was in the evenings and on Sundays when she could be with Maren who always had something amusing to tell.

"You won't believe how busy I have been today,", she said one day after Hannah got home from school, "Ruth is sick so I had to do all the serving and ran constantly between the kitchen and the tables in the restaurant. How they shoot their mouths off! You would think you were in the middle of a monkey and a parrot cage. One of them wanted to call you. They call you 'die Ahna'. They cannot pronounce your name the Danish way. I was chatting with 'the Boot' and 'the Scarf' who wanted to know where you were.' Do you know? ... I have been in love 9 times during the last year and a half. 'The scarf' was the latest. And then he always asks about you!"

Hannah looked at Maren in surprise. Why in the world would Maren's 'Scarf' ask after her?

But Maren continued: "I won't ever marry! I will never again fall in love. Men are just nosebags or foxes or donkeys or wood mites or chatterboxes or gasbags. I would like to smash the water jug, but I can't. It is made of metal. I could cry with rage, but that is such a nuisance. I could choose to run away from it all. I am good enough, when I am clumsy and can make other people laugh by stumbling down the stairs or jump a fence. But nobody really needs me. I could not commit suicide, but I feel like murdering someone."

Suddenly Maren stopped and looked at Hannah: "I don't mean a word of it...so to speak. But your Mother wanted to know why I was grumpy. I could not tell her, because I did not know. I started crying and did that till about 11 o'clock. I hanged up the laundry and there were soldiers teasing me till I wanted to throw the basket at them. Then aunt Hannah came and immediately noticed how 'pissed' I was and almost got mad about it. That was it, so I rushed off and ran up the stairs to my room to cry there. Halfway up I ran into 'the Scarf' who stopped me and asked what was wrong. Which of course I could not tell him. No way was I letting him know that I was in love with him. He is always teasing me. But I think I am over it now. And I will never fall in love again."

"It is not correct to say 'hanged', it is 'hung', came a laconic remark from Hannah after that tirade.

Maren stared at her, completely taken aback, but before she got to utter a sound, Hannah continued:

"Let us go on a bike ride. Your need some fresh air. And I don't want to stay indoors in this nice weather."

They crossed over to the barn to find a couple of bicycles. They only found one bicycle that worked. It belonged to grandfather and was the only one which had real rubber tires, not wood tires.

"We will just borrow it for a small trip", said Hannah, "hop up, I will do the work.

Hannah swung herself into the saddle. Her long legs could just reach the pedals. Maren jumped up behind her. They wobbled off, got a little speed on and reached he road. Then a big blast made Hannah stand on the brake.

"Was that you?" she asked, "I mean the rear wheel?"

Maren already had made a grimace: "Me! Are you mad. The rear wheel exploded!"

She turned around, as a peal of laughter eccoed between the barn and the hotel. It was 'the Scarf' who had witnessed their short trip and laughed so heartily that Maren and Hannah started laughing, too. But it was two very embarrassed girls who went into grandfather to confess that his bicycle had an explosion.

"I will take revenge for laughing at us", said Maren, "just wait!"

Next day when Hannah returned from school Maren grinned: "I got my revenge, I got my revenge! I was washing the floor upstairs, a rare and somber performance, when the door opened and a soldier put his head round the door and said the petty officer wanted to speak to me. I told him that he could go back and report that "The petty officer is crazy." I will never forget seeing the soldier standing to attention and saying: 'I report that the petty officer is crazy!' I could hear a lot of laughter."

Maren paused, then continued: "Unfortunately he came out of the door a little later just as I was carrying the slop pail out. I returned to the loft in a hurry. I don't know why I always have bad luck. It is just horrible that the only water closet in the hotel has been taken over by the Germans. Oh, and you should have seen mrs. Jensen in the kitchen today. She is afraid of mice. She mounted a chair screaming this morning during breakfast when a mouse ran across the floor."

One evening they were all invited to dinner at Knudsen's, the farmer op the road and good friends of Hannah's parents. Maren looked forward to being home alone and then was told, she was also invited. Much to her annoyance. But Mother insisted she come. They were given roast pork and white cabbage filled with minced meat. Icecream for dessert. Maren forgot her irritation and just kept eating.

"Oh, my stomach!" she moaned later, "It is a good thing we can walk home,.."

Hannah and Maren walked arm in arm down the road in the balmy October evening. As usual it was mostly Maren who talked.

"The new maid, Kirsten, has a screw loose. She thinks they are all in love with her. Except 'the Scarf' she says, because he never gives her the time of day. She tried to get his attention by sneaking into his room and pouring water on his face. You should have heard a commotion. Peiter and 'Curlyhead' turned up. I cannot repeat all we talked about. Why the dickens do they have to be Germans. They are really nice guys. Peiter asked if I stayed on when you all move out, and I said I had to stay for a while. I feel like I could ignore propriety, your Mother and public opinion. For some of these guys are really nice. Not all, of course. The Feldwebel is horrible. But the ones I talk with. If we did not have a war, we would all be the best of friends."

Maren suddenly gave Hannah a big hug and turned her around in the middle of the road. Then she continued: "I got so annoyed with aunt Hannah. She called me downstairs and asked me to put on the water for tea and then asked if I was not going to clean the dining room. I may be retarded and an idiot and stubborn and not very intelligent, but I do know how to clean a room. Aunt Hannah apparently does not get it. I had to tell her I could only do one thing at a time. I fear for my sanity (what little I have) if she goes on like this when you have all left. She is so domineering I do not know how to cope with that. I won't go and drown myself, as I have stopped swimming this season."

Hannah laughed:" You are too much!"

"Neither is it a good idea to fall down the stairs, as that happens anyway," Maren continued, 'to go on strike and stop eating will never work. I like food too much. The only thing left is to be grumpy. Let us really enjoy the last few blessed days we have together with good humor, before I get buried under aunt Hannah's colossal wing span. Sjeist die Wandern!"

"Sjeist die Wand an?" Again Hannah was shaking her head grinning. Do you also say this in the restaurant?"

Maren laughed: "I learned it from them. 'Stehenlassen' has a special accent. The is how he makes it sound!"

Maren never held back. She got it all out, either crying or laughing. Hannah loved it and wished she was the one who did not have any inhibitions. Their evening ended with fun and games.

The next day they went to pick Elderberries. The juicy redblack berries would be turned into hot winter toddys and wonderful elderberry soup. Hannah and Maren were enthusiastic and climbed the fences and reached the highest branches to get every single berry. With Maren any kind of work became a wonderful pastime. Whatever they did together was a treat. When they had picked every berry around the house they went up along the road towards Knudsen's farm and picked from all the bushes they found.

"You know I have have had all the eiderdowns out to air and shake today", said Maren, "how annoying we have to move. How annoying that we have a war going on and that there are soldiers everywhere. How annoying that we cannot just stay a normal hotel with normal people coming to stay. If I were God I would finish the war here and now, so your Father and Mother could stay here where they have been so happy and done so well. There are a few powerful grownups who start a war, and then we thousands of normal people have to suffer because of them. That is so crazy.

And I am furious with the 'Scarf' today. He was standing outside with some strange officers I haven't seen before, when I cam wading through a big puddle. I had no idea there was a sewer right there, and that the cover was off. Kasper was just coming round the corner with a shovel when I stepped into it. All the way up to my hip. They all laughed themselves silly over me. I could have killed twice over. Did you know that the 'Scarf' and Peiter have bought a dog? They have named him 'Fellow'. Is is adorable. It ran into the kitchen this morning, when I opened the door. I got him out in a hurry. I did not want your Mother to discover him."

From the road where they were picking elderberries they could still see the fjord. It was so beautiful and calm an evening, but getting dark early now.

"What else have you been doing today?" asked Hannah, "how I wish I could stop going to school now when we have to move anyway. When I have to change school it would make more sense to let me stay home and help here."

"I had a talk with the 'Scarf', it was just good fun. He gave me an elderberry branch for my hair. I will keep it forever. Later I had a long talk with Peiter. I do admire him. It is so amazing he can keep in good spirits in spite of everything. Both his brothers have been captured by the British, his sister was killed in an air raid and his father's business was leveled to the ground by bombs. We talked about the war and did not agree. Only on two points: War is insane, it will soon be over, and England will destroy Germany. Peiter said that he was neither Nazist, Communist or English minded, he just was a logic guy.. I gave him my opinion of the Germans. He insisted they were more humane than the British. I said that noone could be worse than the Germans. He got serious and said he almost wished the British would come here, then I would find out for myself."

Maren looked at Hannah with a sad smile: "I don't mind telling you that I have met two friends I will never forget."

She suddenly looked very solemn when she added: "I am not in love with any of them. I just feel a solid friendship has developed. I have met them because of the war, and I will lose them because of the war. I am sorry I have seen them here for the last time ever."

She spread out her arms in a pathetic gesture. Hannah grabbed her arm and tripped her up, so she would have fallen if Hannah had not kept her up. Maren was getting so serious, I was time to get her to laugh again. Then they giggled all the way home.

The following day rumors had it that a large contingent of soldiers were coming, hundreds of them. The inn would finally be closed completely to the public.

Maren and Hannah grabbed their badminton rackets and went to play on the lawn. Almost immediately a couple of soldier turned up and watched. Maren and Hannah stopped and went round to the parking lot. Two minutes later soldiers turned up there. Then they went down near the river and started playing there. Then Peiter and the 'Scarf' turned up and told them not to be scared, noone would harm them. Maren and

Hannah immediately left again. Nowhere could they play without being bothered by soldiers. Maren talked to the soldiers in the restaurant and in the inn, but it was unthinkable that she would meet and talk to them anywhere else. They gave up and went into the kitchen.

Finally it was their last Sunday in the old house. But it was not a Sunday on which they went to church, or went for a lovely walk in the meadow to pick mushrooms, or went for a walk along the beach and enjoyed their beloved fjord. It was as if all they loved had been taken away from them. Little by little it had been taken over by the war and by the soldiers The fresh air had been polluted by the stench from 'the green men'.

There was barbed wire everywhere, and foxholes and guards everywhere. What had once been a paradise had become a war camp where men came and went, marched and sang their war songs. Where the air was filled with commands and orders and strange war vehicles were on the roads. Soldiers were everywhere, not a spot could one find where there was peace and quiet, where one could be alone in nature.

That Sunday it was not even possible to feel good and cosy in the living room. Everywhere were signs of upheaval. Boxes were filled, things sorted out. Hannah was told to look after the two little ones. Constance was her special little friend, and Tut, the baby was now fun to play with. It was possible to make her laugh so deliciously that she almost regurgitated with delight. Hannah took some children's books and took them into the bedroom where they could sit on the bed and read stories and have a nice time. Kai came and joined them. Then they all sat in their parents big fourposter bed and played and read and laughed.

"Don't you think we could have a sandwich?" Kai looked at Hannah imploringly.

"Me, too!" said Constance

'Why not', thought Hannah; she told Kai to mind the two little ones while she went into the kitchen and asked the cook. Presently she came back with four sandwiches and a plate full of pound cake. She placed the plate in the middle of the bed, so they could sit around it. Oh, how they enjoyed this. Hannah had Tut in her lap and gave her small pieces at a time.

Then Mother came into the bedroom and stopped at the sight. "Honestly, this is too much. You are all sitting in the bed eating pound cake. We will have crumbs everywhere. Hannah, really, you were in charge. Thomas, Thomas!"

She disappeared out the door and they heard her say: "There are 4 naughty children right in our bed."

Father came in and saw his four kids sitting peacefully having pound cake off the plate.

"Trude, Trude, they are siting together, having a nice, quiet time. We know where they are. They are safe. Let us go back and finish what we started."

That was a suggestion to Mother to ignore the crumbs in the bed and the feet on the comforter. They were all going to move. Why did it matter where the children were so long as they were safe and together and had a good time. Hannah drew a sigh of relief.

In the evening Maren talked to Hannah again: "It was crazy in the restaurant. From 2 p.m. on! I have served 28 cups of coffee and a lot of bread and cake. 20 glasses of milk and 30 portions of fried potatoes. They were getting on my nerves. I cannot think when 27 parrots squaw at the same time, even if some of them are nice enough. The 'Scarf' and the Fatman were there for coffee. Then they could not agree about who was to pay for it. The 'Scarf' said I knew in which room the Fatman stayed, and I said that I knew where they both stayed, so they had better pay up. It is basically a good crowd. Peiter said that Ruth had asserted that all Germans were fresh. Did I agree. I could honestly say No. and I told him that your Father had said that of all the companies who had been at the inn, the present was the most well behaved. He was so pleased to hear this and said he was glad we could see that there were decent people among the Germans."

The first moving van comes tomorrow," said Hannah, "I don't know whether to be sad or relieved. I hate to have to start in a new school. But Father says that the hotel is new and very nice and modern, and that perhaps I will get a room of my own. Just imagine! We have been sleeping 5 persons in one room lately. I wish you were coming with us. When will you come?"

"On the first of November. Then the restaurant and the kitchen will be taken over by the Germans. Until then uncle Thomas is responsible for keeping it going. After that it is their own mess. The cook says it has been almost impossible to manage after they took over the scullery. And my Gosh, we have all had to use slop pails ever since the Germans took over the scullery and the only water closet in the whole inn."

Maren suddenly waved both arms about: "But then I will make my entry into Skorsor. Make sure that the town orchestra will play and that the schoolchildren will stand along the roadside with Danish flags and wave at me when I arrive."

Wonderful Maren. She refused to be too serious.

∽

The first moving van pulled up in front of the hotel. Not everything would be moved out today, but all they could do without during the last few days at the Inn. The house became so strangely empty as furniture was carried out.

Maren insisted that the maids had a goodbye party in her room that night. She provided apples and pears and cookies and juice. Oda came and joined them and there was a lot of chatting and laughter and singing and stories. The ones Oda told were mostly off color stories. Ana knew from where she had them. Oda's father liked telling risky stories. Mother would not have approved of them. Maren ran downstairs to get more sodas and juices, and when she came back she said she had run into the 'Scarf' on the stairs. He had stopped her and said he was very sad that he and his outfit also would be leaving the inn, being transferred to the nearest town and then on to the Russian front within a month or two.

"He was terribly sad about it. He has been here for a long time and enjoyed the calm days here. Now he and his small unit may be sent out to be killed at the front. They know that they will not all survive the war. I really feel sorry for them."

But the gloom did not last. Maren could not help herself. Soon it was all giddiness again, and by midnight all five of them fell asleep on the two beds in the room.

The next morning Father and Mother left with Tut and Constance and Ruth. Hannah and Kai had already left for school. Maren helped the family into the taxa that would take them to the railway station.

"You should have seen us," she told Hannah that night, "Oda had played truant, so she was there. We stood together and waved goodbye.

I was bawling, so Oda pulled out a handkerchief and started wiping my eyes. Then I caught sight of the 'Scarf' and Peiter, who stood further away. They started to also wipe each others eyes. It looked so ridiculous that I had to start laughing. We waved the last goodbye and then went into the kitchen and had some of the horrible substitute coffee with some breakfast. Later I met the 'Scarf' on the stairs. He greeted me with a Good Morning. And I took his hand and said Good Morning to him. He asked if we would come and talk to him and Peiter this evening. I said that was out of the question. No fraternizing. But I cannot help liking them. They are so decent, they hate the war, and soon they may be sent out to fight. And they know some of them are bound to lose their lives and will never see their own country again. He asked about you, he always does. I will really miss seeing them. One could not wish for better friends."

Hannah was so absorbed in the life Maren lived that she wished she could just stay home and work with her. She would not miss school for a second. It would be good to never go back. If only she would not have to attend a new school in town. To leave school and work with Maren would have been heaven, she thought. Everything Maren said and did was fun. When she saw the 'Scarf' she could not help stealing a glimpse at him now that Maren had told her he only had eyes for her. What a strange thing.

"Oh, Gosh," snorted Oda, when she heard it, "you are 13 years old! You have never kissed a boy. What on earth could he see in you?"

That was the kind of remark from Oda that sometimes made Hannah withdraw and ignore her. Oda was never loyal. Hannah would never had come with a remark like this to Oda or anybody else, for that matter. It might have been said as a joke, but it was certainly unkind. Hannah turned away from her and talked only to Maren. Oda got the unsaid message and made amends:

"Come on. You cannot help how old or young you are. There is no reason to be sulky. And I have a message from my mother. She wants you to come back with me and stay overnight till you have to leave for Skorsor. Please come!"

Hannah relented: "I can go home with you now, but I have to be back for supper. Grandfather is here."

A little later they took off. On one bike. For Hannah's bike had gone on the moving van. Hannah sat astride the bike and bumped along the short distance to Oda's home.

"My stomach hurts after that bumpy ride," she declared when she got off the bike. A little later she called Oda:

"I started bleeding. Do you have a tissue or some cotton I can use?"

'What bother', she thought, 'why could this not wait another year. It is proof that Our Lord is a man when he inflicts this on women and not on men. It is totally unfair.' she scanned her body, 'at least I do not have prominent breasts like Maren's. I hope they don't get any bigger!'

Hannah walked home. She was not interested in another bumpy ride. She was thinking how impractical it was to have menses. And a few years ago she did not know anything about it. One day little Kai had cried and been afraid and told her he was bleeding when he had to pee and that it hurt. Then Hannah had explained to him not to be afraid. She knew that women would bleed once a month, but she did not know that men also did it. But she had felt so sorry for Kai that she had said in her prayer that night to God, that this was really too much. Was it not enough that women were bothered by this. And then it had turned out, of course, that there was something the matter with Kai that the doctor took care of. And he never had it again. So men did not have menses.

What a nuisance it was. But when she walked home she felt slightly different. She walked with a very straight back and a knowledge that she was not just a child anymore. She thought she carried a deep secret inside her, thinking noone could possibly know. She did not know that her secret revealed itself I her aura, her personal magnetism, which showed others that she was not just a child anymore.

"Did you walk home? Are you crazy? Why on earth?" Maren's eyes were like teacups.

Hannah told her why.

"Welcome to the Red Army, the Danish Women Brigade," Maren opened her arms wide, "oh, how annoying for you, just as you are about to move. What a bother!"

"Is Grandfather here?" Hannah asked. Grandfather represented safety. It was nice to know when he was there.

"Yes, he is. And he and I will leave together. I would much rather stay here. I have come to love this place. And I have no idea what is next. It is maddening. This stupid war. Peiter and the 'Scarf' are also afraid they have to leave very soon. I heard them talk about it in the restaurant"

Maren drew a deep sigh\: "If I were a painter, I would paint the fjord. If I were a poet I would write about all of us here. But I am just an ordinary girl. Or perhaps extraordinary to some. Anyway I can ponder and long for and have wishes. And I do. And I have met two people I shall never forget. They represent friendship and good spirits. Two strangers have shown me that there can still be decency and friendship in a suffering world.

Maren became quite pompous. Hannah laughed:

"You talk about sad things in such a funny way. Sorry I cannot help laughing at you. You should hear yourself!"

Maren recovered somewhat: "I know I say a lot of nonsense. But you know: The grownups are dummer than I. How else can you explain war? War is foolishness. By the way, today I suddenly saw the 'Account'. He turned up and said Hello."

"Who on earth is that? Asked Hannah.

"Oh, you know I just give people names when I do not know what their real names are. He is responsible for paying bills to your Father. I had to interpret for grandfather. He does not speak a word of German. Grandfather is so unhappy on behalf of your Father. To see all their efforts and good work go down the drain to the enemy. Grandfather knows how happy they have been her through all the years. Oh, Hannah! My heart is full. It is your last day here, and soon it is my turn to leave. Then goodbye to this lovely spot on earth, which I have come to love. I have such wonderful memories from here. I cannot weep any more. I have spent all my tears. With complete indifference will I now meet the future. Let it do whatever to me. Nature's free foal will be put in harnish."

All of a sudden Maren could not stand herself anymore: "NO, I will not let anything take away my joy of living. It will always spring forth again."

Hannah just looked at her.

Maren gave her the elbow: "Don't you get it? Here we are, a group of people who under normal circumstances would be the best of friends and do things together. Work as before at this beautiful place and have a wonderful time. But because some idiots have declared war, some of us are not allowed to talk to each other. We, who are just normal people have to put up with that. It is insane. And the German soldiers are even less free than we are. They will be sent to the front whether they want to or not. At least noone can do that to us. When I am grownup I will work for and vote for a United Europe. Everything else is idiocy. That is what I mean when I say that the grownups are dummer than I am."

Maren picked up a floor mat and embraced it and danced around on the floor: "Watch me, this is how all peoples will one day embrace each other and dance together. Nothing else makes sense!"

Suddenly Grandfather stood in the doorway. His handsome face smiled at them. Nobody had such loving eyes as Grandfather, when he looked at them.

"You two gigglers! What are you up to? Come and have some supper."

They had a cosy time with Grandfather, and an hour later Father arrived back from Skorsor. He told them that their apartment in the new hotel was getting in order. The furniture was there and Mother was unpacking. Ruth looked after the little ones and things were going well. Next day the moving van would come for the rest of their stuff, and Kai and Ana would travel with Father.

The last night Ana slept in Maren's room. She went to sleep while Maren was still writing in her diary. She had asked Hannah to take it with her, so it would not get lost in all the commotion.

Early next morning they were standing outside, between the hotel and the beach. They had left the house for the last time. Hannah almost forgot her own misery in her effort to console Kai, who was howling that he did not want to go. She grabbed his hand and talked comforting words to him, while she felt empty herself inside. None of them knew what was ahead. They only felt the pain in leaving the place they considered theirs. They left with a nameless, inexplicable, paralyzing grief inside them. They were pulled up by their roots, and it hurt. Afterwards Ana did not remember how they got to the new hotel, whether by train or bus. She did not know their destination. Things just happened. She had no say. She was almost in shock when she heard Father say: "We are here!"

Hannah looked up and saw a very long, narrow street. They had stopped halfway down the hill. A four story house grew out of the pavement, which was so narrow that only one person could walk at a time. A large gate opened up into a yard where not a green blade of grass was to be seen.

"Dont' just stand there. Help carry in the bags!" Mothers voice cut through her trance. They went into a narrow staircase and up some granite stairs. Everything was clean and neat and barren. Hannah immediately disliked it. They came up into the apartment. There was a large sitting room, a bedroom and a nursery and a dining room with a balcony and a very modern bathroom.

Who is going to be where?" she asked.

"Don't worry about this now. Look after the children, so that Ruth can help me. And when all the kitchen stuff arrives you can help set the table. And then we can also make the beds when Father brings the bed linen and pillows, so we can all get to bed tonight.

"Where will I sleep," Hannah asked, looking almost reproachful at Mother.

"You will be told when Father comes!"

'Oh, how irritating. Why did Mother always refer everything to Father, when Hannah had an important question. Resigned she started playing with the little ones. And when they put their arms around her neck and started giggling she forgot her own anxiety for a while.

Then Father came upstairs and everything became a little easier. Hannah was shown a hotel room, one she might be able to keep as her own. She jumped with delight when she saw it. It was large, had a window towards the street with a view over the rooftops all the way towards a meadow. There was a huge bed, furniture that matched and pictures on the wall and central heating. She had never known such luxury before. Her sorrow over leaving her old home was replaced by her curiosity about all the new.

When she finally got to bed, tired after having helped unpacking, cooking, dishwashing, putting Constance and Tut to bed she pulled out Maren's dairy. She knew she was allowed to read it. On the very last page she read:

"Partir, cet mourir un peu! This beautiful, unforgettable place. I have to leave you soon. You gave me faithful friends. You gave me Hannah and Oda, Ruth and Lis, happy and helpful comrades in good times and bad, for better and for worse. You gave me the friendship of Karl and Peiter, true friends. And you gave me many special and lovely memories. Thank you for it all. I will never forget you. Some day I shall return with my diary tucked under my arm, and when we meet again, beautiful place, my heart will treasure the meeting. Beloved beach farewell and thank you for it all, the good and the difficult. You have forever a place in my heart.

Hannah leafed through some of the pages. Two weeks earlier there was an entry:

"I have to come up for air! I am not crazy. Take it easy. I just have to confide in my diary how much I love Hannah. Never have I adored a girl as I adore her. When I am with her I can not be grumpy, only happy. She is all sunshine. Happy the man who wins her heart. Whatever she might need I will be happy to help her with. I love her. She is just as she should be, not perfect, but full of fun and games."

Hannah smiled and said to herself that this was mutual. She enjoyed being with Maren more than with anybody else. And it had always been that way whenever she came on vacation. Maren thought of doing all sorts of things that Ana was not allowed to do. Like riding on the horses in the meadow last summer. But then it seemed like Maren's mother never told her No to anything. That must be so wonderful.

Maren arrived a few days later and Hannah gave her the tour of the entire hotel. They ended up in Hannah's room, which she was so pleased with. Then with an air of importance Maren said: "I have greetings to you from the 'Scarf'! No, I will call him Karl from now on. He sends his Farewell."

Hannah was one big question mark: "Why? He said goodbye to Father and nodded to the rest of the family, when we left. I did see him out there."

Maren almost bent over with importance: "Can you not get into you pretty head that the most handsome man in the world is madly in love with you?"

Hannah just looked at Maren for a few seconds. This was so weird.

"Honestly Maren," she started, "Father is the most handsome man I know. And I have never exchanged as much as one word with the 'Scarf', or Karl. You know how Oda can chat with anybody. I can't. I usually just stand there and don't ever know what to say. I am also very shy and wouldn't dare. And we are not allowed to. I have only been in the kitchen when the others were there and he came to ask for Father. And when he saved Mother's life by pushing the Feldwebel away. I am too shy to have anything to do with boys."

"He is not a boy. He is a man. He is 24 years old, he told me. That means 11 years difference between you. That may be a little much!" Maren looked pensive, "but I know he is in love with you.

He said you are the prettiest girl he has ever seen, and that when the war is over he will travel back to Denmark and speak to you if you will let him, so you can get to know each other. He said that although you had never talked with each other he knew you were a wonderful girl, for he has watched you the whole year he has been stationed here. And of course I can only agree with him. Besides I promised not to tease him by calling him the 'Scarf' any more, but use his real name, which of course is Karl. But I already told you that."

"Nobody has ever thought I was wonderful. Mother always thinks I am ungrateful or slow or nosey or a fool or..."

Mother's voice from down under called to say supper was ready.

When she crawled under the covers in her new bed, she could not help but think about Maren and the 'Scarf', or Karl as his name was. How unjust life was. There is a man who likes me, but I am not allowed to talk with him because he is an enemy. But I have to be with my Mother who nearly always is dissatisfied with me and scolds me. The world is weird. It should be changed. Why do people hate each other and fight and are mean? Not even in our family which Mother calls 'christian' can we be nice to each other. I did not ask to be born. Since Mother gave birth to me, she should be kind to me, not grumpy or angry. It is not me who owes her something. It is the other way round. I think parents owe it to their children to be nice to them. Otherwise they should not get them.

∽

Hannah started in her new school and was shown where to sit in the classroom. She sat behind two girls who seemed as tall as she was. She was immediately asked a lot of questions.

"I am 16, how old are you?" a girl called Inger asked.

"I am thirteen." Hannah knew she would be asked questions, but she did not have the presence of mind to avoid answering, if she did not want to answer. Others might avoid a question or come with a counter question or say it was nobody's business.

"You are only 13?" Inger spoke unnecessarily loud as if to make everybody listen, "please do this," and Inger lifted her arms over her head and pulled hem backwards, so the contours of her breasts became visible, "you are as tall as I am. I just want to see if you are as well endowed as I am. 13? that has got to be a lie!"

Hannah became so embarrassed that she ignored Inger and asked: "What is the first class about?"

And at the same moment the door flew up and a tall, skinny man entered.

"So, you are the new student! Your name? And date of birth? I want you to move over next to Donde."

And then the information he had about her was related to the class. And she knew she did not like her new teacher. There was no welcome in his ways.

"What is your real name?" she asked Donde.

"It is Hedvig, after a character in a book my Mother was reading when she was expecting me. Don't worry about Inger. She is always so fresh. Do you come from the big hotel in Holmegade?"

Next came their teacher in math. He seemed kind and nice.

"You will find it difficult to follow our curriculum. We use different books and we test in the spring, not in the summer. We may have to give you some extra help."

And so on and on. Horrible to start in a new school.

Little by little the family settled in. Her parents had a business again and she got to know her classmates. There were no soldiers! They hardly ever saw any in town. Hannah got to know her schoolmates. Donde turned out to be a supportive friend. There were two handsome, blond boys in class. They sent admiring eyes to the new girl in class.

Hannah quickly gave up in Math. They had some tests before Christmas, and Hannah had no idea how to solve the sums. Then her teacher told her parents that she needed extra tutoring in order to reach the class level. He came to her home and gave her some lessons, and told her parents that she had a good head. It made all the difference. She was pleased beyond words. Someone had praised her. It did not happen often.

She started getting good grades. An A in Math. And Mother reminded her to be grateful to Father for spending money on tuition. Oh, Mother! She had not asked to change school. That was forced upon her.

Aunt Hannah had good friends in Skorsor. Mr. and Mrs. Robert Willer, whom they got to know well. Robert was director for the local bank and Heddy was his charming wife, who had spent 25 years in America before returning to Denmark to marry her old admirer Robert. Mother and Father, Hannah and Maren got a dinner invitation and went. The apartment was on the second floor over the bank, and Hannah had never seen anything so luxurious as the home she now came into. There were thick, gorgeous carpets on the floors and beautiful furniture. There were the most delicate drapes over the tall windows. They let the light in and yet provided shade from people on the other side of the street. There were paintings on the walls and photographs of friends from different countries. Heddy showed them around and talked about their home and friends. Hannah felt as if she had been transported to a different level of society. She had never before seen such an exquisite home. Heddy talked with grace and authority on all kinds of subjects during the conversation at the dinner table, and Robert told about politics in Skorsor and what had happened in the town. There were beautiful glasses and plates and silverware and Robert served wine, except Mother declined and asked for water instead. She announced her objection to all alcohol and elaborated on the terrible consequences when abused. After dinner they were served coffee and tea in paper-thin porcelain cups.

Hannah was overwhelmed by the beauty of this home. Here she would like to be invited back.

Oda wrote letters to Hannah and asked if she could come and visit. She missed Hannah and wanted so much to be invited. But Hannah did not want to ask Mother if she could come. She also had a hunch that Mother would not want her to come and would say No. And then Oda wrote and invited Hannah to come to her home during the Christmas holiday, saying her parents would be delighted to have her. Hannah showed Mother the letter. And to Hannah's big surprise Mother said Yes:

"That is probably a good idea, just for a couple of days. Then you could bring aunt Hannah and Henriette a nice basket of food and other goodies. And aunt Hannah would be happy to see you. They are doing such an invaluable job for Father by staying at the hotel and managing the phone exchange. They only have the two rooms in the middle of chaos. It must be so difficult."

Hannah got on a train on December 27. The train was slow and there was no heat. After the train she had to take a bus, and finally she arrived at Oda's home. It had been a very cold and unpleasant journey. But she was welcomed with open arms by Oda and her parents. Oda's mother made a fuss over her and really tried to spoil her, and Oda's father made fun with her and teased her, and Hannah loved every minute of it. The day after she arrived she borrowed a bicycle and took the basket down to aunt Hannah. The place looked the same. There was barbed wires around the compound, there were war vehicles and soldiers everywhere. And she had to pass the guard and explain why she wanted to go in. It was a cold and cloudy day and he fjord looked icy and uninviting. Hannah parked the bicycle against the wall next to the hotel entrance and went into the foyer and through the corridor to aunt Hannah, who spread out her arms in a big welcome hug.

"Merry Christmas my darling girl, how are you all? It is wonderful to have you come. What did you bring me!"

And then they unpacked all the wonderful food Mother had put in the basket, and aunt Hannah was jubilant and talkative and loved having her goddaughter liven up the dreary place. She told Hannah that she only spoke French with the officer in charge. She refused to speak German. And that the officers showed her respect. One day she discovered that they had hoisted their Swastica flag on the flag pole in the garden. She had been outraged and demanded of the officer in charge to take it down immediately. That this was a Danish hotel and they had no business putting their flag up! The Swastica was taken down again. Aunt Hannah had a small victory and was proud of it. She told Hannah about her own grandfather who had experienced the war in 1864, when the Germans had won and taken land from Denmark. Noone was more patriotic than she.

Aunt Hannah was around 50 years old and had lived and worked in Switserland and Marocco besides in Danish hospitals. She was heavy and overweight and she could speak with authority, as most nurses who had worked in hospitals were apt to do.

Ana had to tell her all about the new hotel in Skorsor and the visit to

Robert and Heddy, and aunt Hannah asked how Hannah liked her new school, and did she get any new friends? And how was the train ride?

"The train was cold. No heat, it was perishing. It was a horrible wagon rumbling slowly along. At least it is not a long trip. It only took two hours. And there were very few people on board."

They talked and talked and had a lovely afternoon together.

"You must leave before it gets dark," said aunt Hannah, "I think there is a storm coming, I can hear the wind already getting stronger. You must get back in time for supper and before it gets pitchblack outside."

Aunt Hannah sent her off with hugs and kisses and greetings to all. She had to stay near the phone exchange at all times.

Hannah left, went through the corridor and into the foyer. Somebody was there! In the twilight a man stepped out and approached her.

She could have turned around and run back to Aunt Hannah. Or she could have bolted out the front door and not just stood there. But she stood still as if nailed to the floor and just listened to the tender words spoken to her. She let him take both her hands into his, and she just stood there and looked up into his handsome face. And when he put his arms around her and kissed her ever so gently she let him do it. And she melted away in a feeling of bliss, which afterwards seemed to her as if she was not really there. For she had no recollection of how long they stood there, how long the kiss lasted. They had just stood there, as if melted together, until he let her go and said that he would write to her.

She saw a tear in his eye as he squeezed her hand, turned around and left with fast, long steps.

They were enemies in the eyes of the world. But he had done her no harm. Their meeting as two human beings was the most beautiful thing that had ever happened to her.

She got back to Oda's home with her mind in an uproar. Oda immediately sensed something:

"What happened? You are so quiet! Who did you meet? Who did you talk to?"

At first Hannah said nothing. She did not want anyone to know what had just happened. For two reasons. Her thoughts had whirled through her head on the way back. One reason was that it was a shameful thing to have anything to do with a German. It was even a shameful thing to have anything to do with people who fraternized with the Germans. If one talked to a German in any other way that one was forced to, one was a traitor. Father and Mother had to talk to them, because of their business, not because they wanted to but out of necessity. One did not smile at them. One pretended not to see them One pretended they did not exist if possible. One was polite, but never friendly. A girl who fraternized with a German soldier was looked upon as a whore and was called names. It was the lowest one could be. Death seemed preferable to the shame.

That was one reason. And it became more and more clear and formulated in her mind. So one definitely did not tell anyone that one had been kissed by a German. There was no way she could trust Oda. Hannah knew instinctively that Oda would use that knowledge against her if it ever would suit her.

The other reason was that Hannah was deeply moved over what had happened. Maren had told her, that Karl was very much in love with her and found her a wonderful girl. He had been at the hotel for a year and seen her come and go. That any human being thought her wonderful was a miracle. She who was constantly scolded by Mother. And now another miracle had happened. She suddenly knew something about love. It was a pure and beautiful feeling that annulled everything else. It was like a shining pearl. She could not share what had happened to her with anybody. It was too precious an experience.

But Oda did not give up: "Did you talk to aunt Hannah all the time? She pumped her.

"Of course I did. Who else would I talk to!" it was a statement, not a question.

"Did you not see Karl and Peiter? I have talked to Peiter and told him that you were coming. Peiter said, that Karl wanted to talk to you. That Karl is sweet on you."

Hannah snorted with contempt: "Sweet on! How awful!"

She hated that expression. It sounded so cheap. It had nothing to do with what happened between her and Karl. What had happened between them was so incredible and beautiful and vulnerable that noone would be allowed to touch it. She would not share it with anybody.

Oda continued: "I will bet you talked to Karl. What did he say?" she looked expectantly at Hannah. "Perhaps he came in to see aunt Hannah while you were there? He often talks with her. One day I visited her I talked with Peiter in there, and also afterwards outside."

Hannah did not let up. She stayed silent, sat and studied her nails.

"I can tell you a secret if you will keep quiet about it. Peiter and I are sweethearts. And I know that Karl is in love with you, because Peiter told me so. It is not fair of you not to tell me what you were doing. I know you met Karl. How long did you talk together?"

Hannah felt cornered. She never wanted to lie, but she was not going to tell her secret: "He stood in the foyer, when I left aunt Hannah. He said something. It only lasted a moment. I have come straight back from there."

There was a stubborn anger in Hannah's eyes that made Oda stop. It was due not least to Oda's information that she and Peiter were sweethearts. Oda had no reason whatever to go down to the inn and see a German soldier. And at any other time Hannah would have reproached her for it. But now suddenly she could not do that, for she had just herself let a German man kiss her. And what had happened would not happen again. It had been only a short moment. But it had been so incredibly beautiful. Like the Pearl described in the Bible. As if the world had stood still for a moment and had been divinely pure and still and fine.

"Dinner is ready. Come on down!" called Oda's mother. And then they had a delicious warm dinner with meat and potatoes and vegetables and butter.

Oda's father did not want to see margarine on the dinner table. "We live in the land of butter," he thundered with a laugh, "no way are we going to let the Wehrmacht eat it all from us."

At first Hannah had been embarrassed when she heard Oda's father swear. It almost made her feel guilty, when she heard it. Mother would have commented against it, and aunt Hannah would have demanded 10 øre to put in her money box for the Outer Mission. Knowing Oda's father she would probably have gotten it plus a few extra and a few extra swear words for good measure.

When Hannah took the train back to Skorsor she almost felt a kind of panic. Maren would be questioning her about Karl. What could she answer her. Up till now Karl had been a human being, visible at a distance as an enemy, a human being respected as an enemy because he behaved as a decent person, but still an enemy. Maren had worked at the inn, had gotten to know him and said a lot of good things about him. Now Hannah suddenly knew, too, that he was a fine and good human being, besides being handsome as her own beloved Father. But it was forbidden love. She had learned in the Bible that you must love your enemies. But not this way. There was a difference. One did not love one's military enemies. Those one hated and killed and it was O.K. to do it.

And then there was Oda, who had no scruples whatsoever. Oda would never be allowed to diminish her experience to the level of 'being sweet on'. It had nothing to do with being 'sweet on'. It was a pure and fine love without anything bad or wrong mixed in. It could not be destroyed or turned to something ugly.

Hannah arrived with her secret intact. But Maren was as inquisitite as Oda. Only the difference was that she could trust Maren but not Oda. Maren would always be a trusted friend. Hannah told all about her trip and that she had seen Karl, but not that they had met or talked together, that anything had happened between them.

～⌘～

The daily routine started again. Hannah had a lot of homework in her new school, and she had to take lessons to prepare for her confirmation in church in the spring. Once a week she met with some of the other boys and girls at the parsonage for instructions and to lean the catechism. She would celebrate confirmation in April.

Hannah was invited to parties at the homes of some of her schoolmates. Once she went to a party where the parents were not at home. Her classmates were 15 and 16 years old and two of them had brought beer. After they had eaten all kinds of snacks, somebody turned off the lights. A little later when somebody tuned them on again she saw boys and girls in chairs and sofas sitting there kissing each other. She sat alone in a chair and went home determined not to go to anymore of those parties. Donde suggested next day that perhaps she was a little prudish. Hannah answered that she did not want any of those pomaded boys to hold her hand and kiss her. Noone was to get close to Ana. For one thing she was always shy. But what she had experienced with Karl would keep anybody else away.

Heddy would sometimes call Mother and ask if Hannah might come over and help her with small tasks. And if Mother did not need her to babysit for Tut she would go. Hannah loved going there and do whatever little errand Heddy might have for her. They always ended up having tea and delicious sandwiches and cakes, and Heddy often told her that she would have loved to have a lovely daughter like Hannah.

Graceful was a word that Heddy often used. A young girl should be graceful. Hannah felt refined just by going there to visit. Heddy talked about her many years in America and about the many important people she knew there. She made it all sound so exciting and highbrow, almost unattainable.

She had a few poems framed and hanging on he wall between photos. Hannah learned one of them by heart and wrote it down in her newly started diary:

> Im Glück nie stolz sein
> Und im Leid nicht versagen
> Das Unvermeidliche mit Würde tragen
> Das Rechte tun und am Schönen sich freuen.
> Das Leben lieben und den Tod nie scheuen.
> Fest an eine bessere Zukunftzeit glauben.
> Ja – es heisst: Lebe Geist: -
> Dem Tod sein Bittres rauben.

Det mindede hende om Karl og sagde noget smukt og rigtigt om, hvordan man skulle leve.

Heddy told Hannah about books to read. She mentioned Shakespeare and Goethe. She read wonderful Sonnets about love and everything romantic in this world. She mentioned some of the very romantic and dear men she had met and known in America:

"Perhaps some day you will go over there and get married to a delightful young man, who has gone to college and has a good job, and who can show you this gorgeous country."

Hannah would practically float home, dreaming about romantic travels and romantic men. In one of Heddy's romantic novels she read: "The engagement was sealed with a kiss." Then she thought of Karl and wondered if they were now engaged. It seemed so. She would have to wait and see if he came back. Perhaps he would be killed. But it was impossible to think of him being shot. But now she had to be faithful. Even if it was 'forbidden love' in the eyes of others, she would have to be faithful. Mother was very adamant about faithfulness, talked about that. No girl must be like a butterfly, drifting from one to another. Faithfulness between two people was very, very important. But it was all very confusing.

School was not so bad this time around. Now she lived in town and got to know some of the girls fairly well, since she did not have to take a bus to get home. Also she enjoyed a certain admiration, perhaps because she came from the big hotel, or perhaps because her parents knew some prominent people in town. Donde was impressed that she visited the Villers.

"I cannot help that my parents know these people," she did not want Donde to think she felt superior to anybody. Mother's doctrines sat in Hannah's head like beads on a string:

"We are all God's children. Remember you are no better than other people. You must learn humility. You must be a good and obedient servant for the Lord."

Not a day went by when Mother did not quote scripture. Father always said Grace at every meal, and whenever possible Mother wanted a small devotion and a hymn before the children went to bed. And sorry for he or she who dared giggle or come with an irrelevant remark during prayers. Mother demanded respect, preferable submission. She liked to use the term 'Consciousness of Sin'. Her children must know that all were sinners. For Hannah that term suggested that she was worthless, full of errors, guilty whatever she did.

Like everywhere else in the country, many large buildings were occupied by the German Wehrmacht. And so was part of Hannah's school. Almost the only place they now saw German soldiers was in the schoolyard. There was a fence down the middle of it and a guard was at all times walking back and forth there. Most of the children pretended not to see the soldiers. That was their way of showing contempt.

The school building was old and the furniture was old, everything looked old and worn and overused. They were 28 students in her class, too many to get special attention from a teacher. It was not a nice place to go to every day. Ana only enjoyed history and geography, but was not particular diligent. If she was attentive in class she often felt she did not need to do homework. When she did her homework she often sat and daydreamed. Math never became a favorite subject. She would rather practice on the piano. And Mother always had errands for her to do. Or she would look after the little ones.

One day she was called to the phone. It was Fyt, a boy from class. She did not even know his real name.

"I am nearby. Won't you come down. I will be right in front of the hotel."

Reluctantly she agreed. Because she did not know how politely to refuse. She did know that he was interested in getting to know her. He always said Hi and smiled at her in school.

She was hardly down at the front door, before it opened. There was Fyt, a tall, skinny, blond boy.

Hannah just looked at him. She was so shy she did not know what to say, was just one big question mark.

"I would like to go steady with you. I would like us to be together. I would like us to go steady."

Hannah just stared down at the floor. What on earth should she answer. If only it had been Erik who had asked. She liked Erik who was incredibly handsome and tall and blond. But she was not interested in getting to know Fyt very much. His begging eyes were enough to turn her off. And what did it involve to 'go steady'?

"I don't want to go steady with anybody!" she stammered out.

She saw the Adam's apple in Fyt's throat go up and down. He said something, but she did not get it. Then he was gone.

Hannah drew a sigh of relief. Whatever she had avoided, it was a relief. And she did not know what it would have involved if she had said yes to Fyt. She had seen boys and girls sit and kiss each other at one of the parties she had been to. She did not like that. And Mother would strictly have forbidden it if she had known. And to 'go steady' with a boy' sounded also like something Mother would never have allowed. Besides there was Karl. In a way she now belonged to Karl.

Grandfather came to visit. Dear, wonderful Grandfather. His eyes were so loving, his smile so gentle. You were always safe with Grandfather.

Little Grandmother never came. She was old and weak. Ten years older than Grandfather, who was 70 and still used his bicycle to get around.

Father and Grandfather often sat and reminisced. That day Hannah heard them talk about a new bicycle Father had managed to buy a year ago. These days it was almost impossible to get hold of a new bicycle. Father had it back at the fjord hotel when they still lived there. And when Grandfather had come to visit them Father had given him the new bike. So when he left to go home the old bike stayed in the carriage house.

Dorothea's son had seen both bikes and had asked Father if he had made a good deal when doing the exchange.

And Father had answered: "We just switched bikes!"

To which Dorothea's son with exasperation in his face had exclaimed: "But that is crazy. Then you have really been taken advantage of!"

And then Father and Grandfather laughed so happily it was impossible not to join in.

That day Hannah was helping Mother cook dinner and Constance was told to set the table. Father sat at one end of the table and Grandfather at the other end. When they had finished eating soup Grandfather held up a large serving spoon and said with a smile: "It is rather a large spoon for eating soup!"

"Constance!" Mother looked at her in reproach, "What were you thinking?"

"HeHe", Father started laughing, and soon all the children joined in. Grandfather's eyes were filled with mischief. Hannah just loved him. It was so typical of Grandfather. First he put up with eating from a much too large spoon, and then made fun of it afterwards. And he was so modest. He was not going to ask anybody to leave the table to get him another spoon. Only he loved to share what was funny with the family.

Why did Mother not have a sense of humor? Good thing that Father had started laughing, before anybody was scolded. And little Constance sat there with a happy grin on her face, when she realized that she was the reason they all laughed. She enjoyed being the center of attention.

Two weeks later while Father was away Mother told the children that Grandfather was ill at home. He had pneumonia and this was very serious. One might not survive this. They should all pray for Grandfather. Hannah helped getting the little ones to bed. They sat in their nighties and Constance began: "I am tired and will go to bed, close my eyes and go to sleep, Look with love upon me down, dearest God and ….."

At that moment Mother came in and said: "Father can not come and say goodnight this evening. He is with Grandfather. You must pray for him. He is very ill."

There was something in Mother's voice that was scary. For the first time it dawned on Hannah that Grandfather might actually die. That was terrible. He had just been with them. Well and in good spirits and full of fun. Hannah went up to her room and prayed and prayed to God to take care of Grandfather so he would not die. But something inside her felt that perhaps it was to late to pray. Mother had sounded so serious.

Three days later Father came home and told them that Grandfather had died. The house became very quiet. Noone said anything. Hannah felt like paralyzed. When she walked around the house she concentrated on paying attention to the others and not to do anything wrong. Bodil came home, very unhappy, so they could hardly talk about it. Maren came and was talkative as usual. But when she talked about Grandfather she started crying. A little later she might say something funny. Hannah felt better in her company. If Maren could be her own self, she did not have to be so scared of doing or saying something wrong. Mother and Father were busy helping arrange the funeral, manage the hotel and take care of the little ones.

Then the day arrived when they all went to the funeral. When they came to the farm, there were already at least a hundred people. Grandfather had been known all over the country. Hannah saw her cousins and aunts and uncles and little Grandmother. Grandmother seemed smaller than ever, as if she had shrunk further because of losing Grandfather. Hannah had never played with Grandmother as she had with Grandfather, but she had sometimes sat next to her and learned to cart and spin. For Grandmother had her own sheep and used the wool from them. Now she was 80 years old.

"Come and say Goodbye to Grandfather, children," said Mother quietly. And they went with Mother and Father over to the coffin in the middle of the yard. There was Grandfather in the large white coffin, looking as if he were asleep. His eyes were closed and he looked so nice, as he always did. Hannah's eyes filled with tears. She looked at his hands.

They were large and broad and looked a lot like Father's hands. She stole a look at her own hands. They looked the same, except they were smaller.

Now Grandfather had died, because he was old and became sick, but Father lived on and so did the rest of the family, and Hannah lived on. Grandfather looked the same, but his spirit had left him. It was so very strange.

While she stood there looking at Grandfather she felt it was good and a natural thing to stand here and think Goodbye to him. She did not say anything loud or touch him. She felt others were watching her. Otherwise she would have liked to put her hand on his, just to touch him one more time. But in her mind she said goodbye and at the same time felt that Grandfather would always be near her, if she needed to feel safe, and because she always would be able to remember him, remember his gentle, lovely laughing eyes and his goodness. When she moved away from the coffin she was glad she had seen Grandfather. She had said Goodbye to him. She couldn't have, if she hadn't seen him.

It was a large gathering that followed the coffin, first to the church service, then on to the grave. Before the coffin was lowered down into the earth several men in black coats and hats made speeches about the many good deeds Grandfather had done. Apparently he was known by people all over the country. Little Grandmother stood there with red eyes, full of tears.

When Father helped lower the coffin down into the earth she saw tears ran down his cheeks. Oh, how much he must have loved him. Hannah suddenly felt alone and wondered if anybody would ever love her that much.

༆

One day on her way home from school Hannah stopped at the top of Holmegade, the long street where the hotel was. She stood completely still and just looked and looked. Up the hill came a strange procession towards her. First an old woman clad in dark clothes, old rags it seemed, and a scarf around her head. She was pulling a small cart on which sat some bundles, it must be children. And behind her more figures. They all seemed to struggle to walk up the street, leaning forward as if about to give up, moving slowly and almost mechanically.

In a split second she knew that they must be fugitives. No Danes looked like that. They must have come from another country. How on earth did they get across the border? What did they get to eat? Where did they sleep? How did they manage?

The questions raced through her head. The woman came closer and closer without so much as lifting her head and looking up. In a whirlwind of thoughts she imagined what these people must have left. She herself had lost her home. She had felt almost paralyzed when she left the fjord hotel. But she had a new home. She had not walked for miles like a beggar without knowing where she would end up. Silent, dark figures moved towards her. They had no rights, came from a foreign country. But they seemed to forewarn her, like a threat that crept closer. Messengers about an evilness that touched her and pierced her conscience.

Suddenly she ran. She bolted down to the hotel, ran through the door and up the stairs and into their apartment, into the nursery where she threw herself down on the bed and started sobbing, shocked and horrified.

"What on earth is the matter, child?" Mother came in, worried about the way Hannah had arrived.

Hanna sat up and turned towards her with tears running down her face:

"Look down the street, Mother," she almost screamed, "look how they are coming up the street."

Mother rushed to the window, stood still and put her hand against her chest: "May God have mercy upon us."

The words stumbled out of Hannah's mouth: "Look how poor they are. They have nothing. Where do they come from? Who are they? Where are they going to live? Somebody must help them. They cannot just keep going. They must have a place to live. And something to eat."

As always she could not stand to see anybody suffer. Then she suffered with them. She could not stand injustice. Somebody had to help them.

She did not have to wait long for the solution.

A few days later Father told the family they would have to move again. He had been told by the authorities that the hotel would be expropriated to house refugees. They could stay in their apartment, but the rest of the hotel would be off limit to them.

Father's protest was in vain. Their four year old modern hotel would be more or less destroyed by lack of care. And their business once again ruined. They would have no income, only whatever they might be paid in rent.

Father did not want to stay and once again have his family live among strangers, whether they were refugees or the military. He had to find a solution for them.

"Are we refuges now?" asked Hannah when they were told at suppertime, "where will we go?"

Mother turned towards her with a disapproving look: "Trust in God who will give us food and clothes tomorrow as He did yesterday!"

Hannah remembered the quote from the Bible about the Lilies in the Field and she just looked down at the tablecloth.

Then Father said: "We may borrow aunt Ellen's summer house till the war is over."

Hannah looked up and with enthusiasm beaming out of her face, she said: "Really? That is a lovely place!"

All of a sudden all worries were as blown away. Hannah remembered aunt Ellen's summer house. It was not just a small cottage, it was a large, beautiful house called Skovly. What a wonderful solution. The refugees got their hotel and in the meantime they were going to live in a lovely place near the water. None of them would be homeless. The economic problems this would cause Mother and Father did not enter her mind. She was used to not having any money. Always they had to be frugal. That was normal.

Before they left town Mother took her shopping. She was going to be equipped properly for her big day, the confirmation in April.

For the first time in her life, Hannah got a new coat. It was made of something other than wool or cotton, which was not available. It was actually a kind of paper, said the shopkeeper. But the coat looked very smart and Hannah was happy. They also found a fine brown hat to go with it and a dress for the day after the confirmation, when there also would be visitors and a party. The dress she was going to wear in church for the ceremony was a white dress, changed from one of Mother's from the 1920'is. It had a real Brussels lace collar, which had been on Mother's wedding dress and Hannah thought it was beautiful.

So once again they packed many of their belongings and left the apartment. Father locked it securely, as some day they would return to it. When they arrived at the summer house it was almost as if they were coming to a small castle, thought Hannah. They arrived late afternoon in twilight and drove up towards a large, white house, that seemed to shine in the evening light. It was built of wood and painted. It had no central heating, was meant for summer living only. They entered the back door into a large kitchen that expanded into a dining room and on to a veranda, from where they could see a large lake and wooded hills beyond. From the dining room you could go left into a library with many books and a piano, and further in to a large sitting room. Beyond that there were two bedrooms and a bathroom, connecting to a large foyer and the front door, and from there one could go upstairs to the second floor where there were three bedrooms, and then further up to the third floor where there were two bedrooms.

The children entered the house almost in awe. This was so much nicer than the modern hotel in town. And within minutes Kai and Hannah stormed through every room in the house, then out in the garden where a large heather lawn was surrounded by dusty paths. They found benches among flowers and bushes, a boathouse near the lake shore and a couple of canoes. It was almost spring. There were daffodils and crocus and budding trees.

It was a paradise to come to. Spring was in the air. It was wonderful to be in the countryside again. Who wanted to live in town? Oh, to smell the earth!

There was only one annoying thing for Hannah. She had to go to school again. She was to attend aunt Ellens school in town, so every morning she went on bicycle almost ten kilometers. Not that she minded the ride, for it was beautiful during the woods. But it just was not pleasant to change school.

The good thing was that she did not have to mix with the other students after school. There were no embarrassing parties with boys making passes at her. She rode her old bike in rain and wind and sunshine and felt happy to be back in the country. Mother was not always angry. All of a sudden she did not have much to do and grew milder and kinder. She was away from the inn, from work, from Germans soldiers and worries. No hotel guests, no threats from informers. For the first time in many years Mother was just a housewife, a whole new relaxed way of life for her.

Every weekend aunt Ellen came with her cook and a maid and food and took over the household and brought excitement into their lives in the form of books, grammophone records and good spirits. One day she brought and introduced a Mr. Svendsen.

"He is one of my dear summer guests," she said at the dinner table one Saturday night, "he will stay in the empty room on the third floor for a few days.

So he stayed when aunt Ellen went back to town. And he stayed and stayed.

"We do not comment on his staying here," Father said.

And then that was an implied agreement. Hannah and Bodil knew not to mention him.

The children hardly saw Mr. Svendsen, But one Saturday when Bodil was home for the weekend she mentioned to Hannah, that they only saw him at night when he left the house around 9.30 and they never saw him come back. They knew from newspapers and from listening to grownups that there were saboteurs in the area, and they often heard explosions from the directions of the railway that ran from the the north of Denmark to the border with Germany.

"I will bet he is a saboteur," said Bodil

Hannah's eyes grew big with surprise: "Do you think he is a saboteur?"

"Yes, of course. Why else would he be here? He must have gone 'underground'"

Bodil and Hannah began to show interest in Mr. Svendsen's whereabouts.

"Is Mr. Svendsen here," they might ask at breakfast.

"He sleeps late," was the usual answer.

They were never told, but Mr. Svendsen now had two faithful admirers who were interested in his life and welfare. They would have denied any knowledge of him had they been asked. And they always sent him a smile if they ran into him. They stayed quiet and loyal and found it exciting that he stayed in the same house as they did. If they missed seeing him a couple of days they got worried. But if they asked about him, they were never told.

"He comes and goes as he pleases," said Father.

They never mentioned him to anybody, not even to Kai. Kai was so young he might inadvertently say something.

It was a wonderful spring. They had a carefree time, the house hidden away in the woods near the lake. The older children went to school. Mother and Father had no work to do. It was like being on vacation. There was still a war raging, but it did not touch them as it had done before. There might occasionally be soldiers on the roads and in the woods, but they were not bothered by them on a daily basis as before. They did not come near the summerhouse. When the children came home from school Mother had tea and goodies for them. She was usually in good humor. She would even play badminton with them. It was a whole different daily routine. She had time for her children. Life seemed safe and good. Aunt Ellen came out on weekends and had Bodil with her. Once her brother from Copenhagen came with his family, and the conversation at dinner table was animated and interesting beyond anything Hannah ever had listened to before.

Hannah's confirmation a Sunday in April became a lovely family party. In the morning was the ceremony in their church in Skorsor. Father had hired a taxi to take them all back and forth from and to Skovly. It was an expensive affair. Driving out of Skorsor over the meadows outside town no one mentioned the terrible accident that had happened there a few week earlier. But Hannah thought about it. Erik's mother had been killed there. In a very rare accident. She had been in a taxi which had been mistaken for a car with German officers when a Royal Air force plane had spotted it and opened fire. It was so strange to know this had happened to someone she knew.

There were 15 people around the table in Skovly. Aunt Ellen had decorated it with spring flowers. Many family members had been invited but only few had been been able to come. It was an uncertain time with slow trains or canceled trains.

During dinner and between courses there were songs and speeches in her honor. Hannah smiled and said thank you and hardly knew how to behave. She was not used to being the center of attention. She received beautiful gifts, a gold watch from Godmother, a carved sewing box from uncle Helge and a beautiful necklace with an amethyst and small diamonds by aunt Ellen and so on.

Aunt Ellen was always interested in the children. She taught several classes at school and was very interesting to listen to. She also played the piano and would gather the youngsters for singing.

"You have a lovely soprano!" she said to Hannah.

To Mother she said: "It is a treat to have your lovely daughters at my school."

Mother answered with a cutting remark: "Please do not mention it. We do not want them to be conceited."

But aunt Ellen did not stop. "I am sure they won't be. Bodil is a brilliant student, the best math student in our High School. And Hannah is a lovely girl who carries herself well."

Hannah loved it. Here was a grownup who with a natural authority aired an opinion different from Mother's.

Maren had a job back in Skorsor with a landscaper, but she came once in a while, as her parents lived within walking distance of Skovly, so she and Hannah often went for walks in the woods. Maren's father, uncle Cristen, and Thomas would often meet and sit and talk about old days and have some wonderful laughs together. But there were also scary news about young freedom fighters who got caught and got shot by the Germans. Then Fathers face was like a thunder cloud: "When will it ever end?" he would say, "the war will soon be over, but they still shoot our young men.".

On May 4th when Hannah and Mother started clearing the table after supper Father turned on the radio to listen to the news. All of a sudden they heard the announcement that the German forces in Belgium, Holland and Denmark had surrendered, capitulated...Hannah could not repeat exactly the words when she told uncle Christen. It had been as if time suddenly stood still. Just for a moment. Then they all jumped up with joy.

"Hurray, hurray, Hannah, run over to uncle Christen and ask him, if they have heard the news. And tell him to come and bring the family."

Hannah bolted our the door and ran across the road and the railway. She danced and floated as if on air. The beech trees were going green.

Forsythias were in bloom and stood yellow and proud. Tulips were up and the earth smelled delicious. All of a sudden the world seemed beautiful and perfect. No more war. Imagine, it was over. It was like a new chapter in a book. Hannah ran into the small house through the back door, through the kitchen and into the sitting room where uncle Christen sat with his wife and youngest daughter.

"Have you heard? Have you heard? We are free. They have just said it over the radio. The war is over!"

It was impossible for Hannah to stand still. She stood there and jumped up and down. Uncle Christen and aunt Sidsel sat in each their armchair while she stood there almost dancing.

First uncle Christen looked at her as if not understanding. Then his face turned into a broad, happy smile.

"The Germans have capitulated, From tomorrow morning. In Belgium, Holland and Denmark. Father says to come over to us and celebrate."

Hannah was still hopping up and down. "Will you come, Uncle Christen, shall I help you with aunt Sidsel?"

Her face beamed down towards aunt Sidsel, who could not walk without a cane. Uncle Christen's head was round as a balloon and almost bald, like Grandfather's had been. And his smile seemed to go all the way back to his neck when he said: "God be praised, God be praised!" His wise eyes looked at Hannah who was tripping like a foal in the stable when smelling green grass in the meadow.

"Aunt Sidsel and I will take it easy and come in a little while. You run home and tell them we will be there soon. But be careful crossing the road. On a night like this we don't know how the Germans may react. So you watch out!" And he added: "Thanks and Praise be to God. May we have lasting peace now!"

Hannah danced home again and jumped the fence to the garden. Mother and Father were happy. Everyone was happy. She wanted to sing all the lovely songs she often played on the piano about the beauty of the Danish landscape. She danced into the house and grabbed Kai's hands and started whirling him around while she sang an old war sang from an earlier war with Germany: "When once I went to war, my girl would come along!..............."

Mother came in from the kitchen, smiling: "I think that is enough. Help put Tut to bed. And then we will have coffee and cake when we all sit down."

Hannah lifted Tut who was getting heavy and danced into the bedroom with her. "Now I will tell you a story," she said, and while she got Tut into her nightie she told about the Sandman who came with his umbrella and made little children sleepy. However, there was too much excitement in the house for Tut to be sleepy. Hannah brought her back to the living room and she eventually went to sleep there while the grownups sat and talked about the five evil years they had been through and now were a thing of the past. Father said prayers and thanked God that Denmark did not turn into a battle field, but could celebrate freedom from occupation. And they sang some hymns before turning in.

Next day uncle Christen came over with his horse and carriage, and they all went to town. They had decorated the carriage with green branches and flags. The town was celebrating. People were out in the streets on this beautiful spring day, talking to each other whether they had met before or not. The whole country was celebrating. Freedom fighters turned up with armbands showing they no longer had to hide what they had been doing. There were also English and American flags and talk about the day the British would come through town. One of Hannah's school mates told her that her father had been in the resistance movement without her ever knowing anything about it. It was a day never to be forgotten. When they got home they learned that Mr. Svendsen's name was really Vestergaard and that he truly had been a saboteur and had gone underground and now would be going home to his big farm on Fuhnen.

∽

There were talks about traitors and those who had made money by working for the Germans. There would be a day of reckoning. There were girls who were caught in the streets and held by some while others cut off their hair. That was punishment for having fraternized with German soldiers. Hannah saw one of them and was terrified. The girl was almost bald, only a few tuft of hair was left. How humiliating it must be.

Finally the day came when British troops came to town. The children were not at school. They stood along the road side and saw the military vehicles come slowly through the streets. Their uniforms were different from the Germans, and they were greeted with flags and shouts of joy. Denmark was free again and thanked their liberators by showing their enthusiasm wherever they could.

∞

The family moved back to the hotel in Skorsor a few monhs later. But first the authorities had to build baracks for the fugitives. Some of them went back to their own countries, others did not. A whole group from Lituania did not want to go back. They feared the Russians. And when Mother and Father saw how much damage had been done to the hotel, they were very discouraged. However, they got the hotel going again and had repairs done. A receptionist was hired to welcome guests and a cook came to be in charge of the kitchen. At one point Hannah was asked to help as a waitress. Mother thought she needed to pitch in. She did, but she did not like it, for there were male customers who came with complementary remarks, and once somebody patted her behind as she walked by their table. When Father heard that, it was the end of Hannah helping in the restaurant.

Hanna somehow managed to catch up with examination requirements at school, although she had been away for months. Her friend Donde would help with Math, if ever she needed it. Donde loved to visit her at the hotel. One day when they walked in the front entrance, Donde started talking to Peter, the young man who was hired as the receptionist. Donde could chat with anybody, and her green eyes were very inviting. She was a natural flirt. She did not put it on, it was just the way she was. But that day Mother came down at the same time Hannah and Donde were chatting with Peter.

"What are you doing here? You are not supposed to be here. Peter is at work, has to do his job. Don't stand here and disturb him with your foolishness. Hannah, you should know better. Perhaps it is time we send you to boarding school."

"I would like that very much!" Hannah blurted it out without thinking. But it was true. Bodil liked being there, and to get away from Mother would be just great. Here she was always under her thumb, never good enough, often shamed for one thing or another. It would be heaven to be away. But Mother never used that threat again.

One day when things became really bad between her and Mother, she burst into tears and could not stop. She cried and cried and finally Mother called Heddy and asked her for help, saying that Hannah was in a bad shape and she did not know what to do with her, and could she possibly spend some time with Heddy. Within half and hour Heddy was there and persuaded Hannah to come home with her. Heddy said she could use her help and afterwards they would have a nice dinner and then go to the movies, and Hannah could spend the night there. Hannah agreed, still crying, and they left together.

Heddy did not pry into whatever made Hannah so miserable, just asked gently if things were too difficult at school or at home. And Hannah, still sobbing, said that she could never be good enough, that Mother was always annoyed with her and told her to be ashamed. She just did not know how to be.

Heddy had Hannah help her prepare dinner. They had lamb chops with mint sauce and green peas and scalloped potatoes. And for dessert fresh fruit and icecream. Robert came up from the bank and was very attentive and told funny stories. Heddy showed Hannah the lovely guestroom she would sleep in. It was all in pale blue and white with orange lampshades. A room for a princess. And then they went to the cinema and saw Waterloo Bridge, which made Hannah cry all over again, because it was so sad. And Heddy said when they left the cinema, that she would certainly have chosen another cinema, if she had known how sad the film ended. But Hannah said she loved the movie, it was just a sad ending. And she thanked Heddy for giving her a lovely time and added that she had to study hard for her exam now, and how difficult it had been to change school so often. "Everything is just so hard right now. And I never know when Mother is annoyed with me!"

"Let me tell you something," said Heddy, "you only turned 14 in January. You are somewhere between child and grownup. That can be a very confusing and difficult time. And then when a woman gets into her 'forties' she is also going through some changes and can have a difficult and confusing time. We call it Menopause. Perhaps that is where your Mother is right now."

Hannah looked at Heddy. "Then she has been in it a long time!"

That winter they had quite a lot of snow. Hannah's school mates went skiing in the woods outside town, and some of her friends wanted Hannah to come with them. Hannah pleaded with Father and Mother to give her a pair. And she got them for Christmas. It was wonderful to be in the fresh air and slide over the white snow. And then after Christmas Father again gathered the family and announced that when spring came they would move again. He had been offered to run a large farm on Fuhnen and had accepted it. However modern the hotel was, it could not compare to life in the country. They had never lived on a street before. Life in town was not attractive to him and Mother.

The children were excited when told they would soon be living on a big farm with cows and horses and pigs and chickens. So much better than living in a town.

Hannah would stay in Skorsor till the end of the school year and she had passed her exams. Heddy had offered to have her stay with her and Robert till she had acomplished them in June. Maren still had a job in town, and they saw each other once in a while, but Maren was very involved in the local Y.W.C.A. and saw young people her own age. It was not a daily gettogether as at the inn. But one day she called Hannah and said they had to meet. It sounded urgent. When they met, Maren's face was one big qestion mark.

"See what I have here!" and she produced an envelope with a strange stamp on it, "what is inside is also for you! Why did you not tell me about you and Karl?"

At first Hannah did not understand what she was talking about. Then Maren explained:

"I had given my address to Karl before we moved from the inn. Remember he wanted to come back some day when that was possible, if he survived the war. He did, Hannah. This letter is from him. There is a letter for both of us. But you never told me you two had talked together. You have kept that a secret."

Hannah looked at the envelope before she took out a letter from inside. On the back was an address: It said: Karl Ortman, Hohenzollernstrasse 8, Recklinghausen.

Somehow time seemed to stand still. Deep inside Hannah's mind was a small shining light. She had grown up with a Mother who never gave her a hug, hardly ever praised her, mostly shamed her and abused her. And in the midst of this devastating war somebody from the other side had shown her love and had cared about her. Had wanted to be with her. And it had been so precious she had not been able to share it with anybody. But now Maren knew that something had happened.

Hannah looked lost. "Maren," she said, "I hardly know him. And I can hardly speak German, only what I have learned in school. Nor can I write letters. It was just something beautiful that happened. I just want to remember it. I would not know what to write."

Maren threw out her arm in a gesture of amazement: "Aren't you going to read this before you say anything? Are you not curious?

Hannah took out a sheet with a strange handwriting and started reading, then moved close to Maren so she could read at the same time :

"Help me read it, she said, "the writing looks so different with those oldfashioned letters."

Maren started reading: "Liebe Hannah..." then she paused and said, "let me see. I think they are called Gothic letters, and because the verb usually comes at the end of a sentence, it makes it so much harder to read. Listen! He writes that he and Peiter both survived the war, but that he was wounded at the Eastern front and …..he writes that coming home was both good and bad. Bad because whole sections of towns have been bombed and turned into gravel. The task of rebuilding seems overwhelming….. That it will be many years before Germany can completely recover. And…..he feels so bad for his country that once produced men like Schiller and Goethe and Mozart and Beethoven and many other great men, but today the German people are hated by the world because of Hitler and his horrible gang….Then he goes on to thank you and me. He says that in the middle of this horrible war the only good thing was the time he stayed at the fjord hotel and saw you and Maren….. me., that is…..and that he will always remember that year as a peaceful time ….and blessed. He is grateful that his unit was the most well behaved according to your Father….. he writes that seeing you grow into a very beautiful young woman was something he will always remember, and that there will always be love in his heart for you. That you are so young and must be free to embrace life and be able to pursue your dreams whatever they are, ….and never experience another war. And that you will always remember…. "….." and that one day our two countries can show friendship and………..

"Oh, Hannah, is it not wonderful that they survived! I am so happy for them. But how awful to come home to a destroyed country. And he does not say how badly he was wounded.

Hannah finally confided in Maren that for a brief time in the foyer she and Karl had met and he had said many loving words to her.

"But Maren, there is no way I can receive letters from him, What would Mother and Father think and say? I have not told anybody. Besides I can not write in German. You will have to decide what you want to do……!

∽

For the rest of her life Hannah remembered those few moments in the dark house near the fjord as the most pure and beautiful meeting ever. It was almost like a shield against evilness, like a gift that could not be taken away from her. A love given with tenderness in a hateful world. She never saw him again, but she never forgot and she was forever grateful for that moment in time.

It was point counter point in her life, although she did not know how to express that.

∽

Hannah once said she had made milestones in her life. She did not often share what hurt her. She would observe others, learn and wonder. When she was hurt she withdrew into herself. When she was abused as a child she mostly just stood there, silent, afraid, and with questions in her eyes. She was not broken, only silenced. For if she answered back she might get hit or abused verbally even more. Her conscience seemed to convey that she was nothing but also that she was something. For there were people who loved her without hurting her. That helped her survive injustice and betrayal. Her experience of betrayal of a mother's love was what she never understood. How could one hurt and punish a person one loved? How could anybody be indifferent, treacherous and false towards a person one purported to love? Hannah's soul, her center of gravity, her innermost thoughts were within her as something no one could take away from her or touch. She survived on this for many years, when life was difficult and in acute moments when she thought of ways to end it all, and if she would ever do that which she knew she would not; just play with the idea. She had learned to bend like a willow branch in the wind and she never wanted to relive her childhood. There were surely good times in between, but they were lived spontaneously, while the bad times were like prints on her soul.

Her mother was forever a mystery to her. Her mother had a sincere wish to be a good and decent being. She prayed every day to God. She did help many people. Why could she not control her temper and be loving towards her pretty and gifted daughter? What kind of mindset is jealous?

When her mother was in her eighties she once said to Hannah: "You are very much like your father, calm and caring. You must forgive me. I know I was not always nice to you. I was jealous of you."

Hannah had been so surprised she could not even comment on that. She just wondered how a mother could be jealous of her daughters instead of being proud and happy for them, jubilant that they were doing well. Surely a daughter's success reflects back on her mother.

However, if a child has repeatedly been verbally abused and lost her self esteem, she may never quite recover from that. A word said can not be taken back, and an apology does not erase the effect it had on you.

Hannah had a long life, and eventually a happy life. By nature she was a happy, mischievous girl. She was pretty and had this 'comehither look' in her eyes that some are borne with. She was tall and slim with a lovely figure and was good at whatever she put her mind to.

Denmark may be the only country in the world that has a 'Jantelov', or 'Jantelaw'! It consists of 10 sentences and was created by Aksel Sandemose, and author who grew up in a small provincial town in Denmark. On the house where he was born is a placard with all ten sentences. Every sentence in the 'Jantelov' is a 'put down'. He moved to Norway and stayed there throughout his life. Here is an example of the 'Jantelaw': "Do not think you are anything special! Do not think you are better than the rest of us! Who do you think you are?" etc.etc.

So much for 'Happy Danes'! Jealousy thrives there as well as anywhere else.

Hannah left home and saw other family patterns. She knew she wanted to become independent and do her own thing. But patterns are hard to break. She constantly fell under the influence of others who voiced their opinions and told her what they thought she should do. Finally she met and married her beloved Alan. They lived well. They traveled all over the world and had a wonderful life. Hans Christian Andersen said in his story, 'The ugly Duckling', that if you are a cygnet, it does not matter if you grow up in a duck pond. You will eventually grow up to be a swan. Of course Hannah knew that story and never gave up hope that things would turn out well.

So in spite of her difficult relationship with her mother, she was privileged. She had a wonderful father and grandfather, who were caring and fair and well balanced. They were like safe anchors in a tumultuous world. And she remembered the mostly poor people in the fishing village as upright and decent and kind. She saw people who had common sense and were able to live good lives. She knew it was possible to live a happy, harmonious life and never gave up her faith in goodness. She left this world a happy woman, grateful for her children and the many dear people in her life.

⌒◯⌒

Before she died a wise old woman I asked Hannah what she had learned. She said: "I have shared all this with you for one reason only. If it can help just one woman to stand up against abuse and manipulation I have not shared it in vain. It was not the war as such that had a lasting effect on me. It was my mother's far too strict upbringing. Our own private war. Our country was occupied by foreigners. My mind seemed occupied by my mother and her demands.

I was a very naive child, brought up listening to Christian doctrines from my mother and the society we lived in. I never understood why my mother and Oda and my first husband and some others were annoyed or jealous of me and in their conduct sought to either run my life or discredit me in my own eyes as well as in the eyes of other people, in Oda's case take advantage of me by clinging to me in order to gain access to my friends and family, and at the same time be disloyal to me. I did not understand it was jealousy till my mother told me she had been jealous.

Then it dawned on me that this had happened for other people, because I was pretty or smart or for whatever reason.

I grew up in a pattern of behavior that was like a cage I could not get out of. I was supposed to be nice and kind and understanding, and also to be obedient to my mother. So I was obedient even when I thought it was unfair. I hoped for peace, for the common sense and reason my father always projected. But I was not smart enough to put that into words or eloquent enough to debate what seemed unreasonable or even outrageous to me. I put up with things and accusations, often without protest. For I was brought up to know I was a sinner, an egoistic girl who should be ashamed. I have been ashamed much of my life, although a little voice inside me told me not to be, told me that I was O.K., that in fact I had little to be ashamed of. That I was more reasonable than the ones accusing me. Shaming me made me very shy with people I did not know well.

Before I married my first husband I had no idea that anyone could be brilliant and deceitful at the same time. But he was.

He told me I was wonderful and swept me off my feet. And once we had married he wanted to decide everything. My first marriage was one long period of putting up with lies, making excuses for him, giving in as I had given in to my mother and other people. I gave in when I was in an emotional situation with someone, who told me that I was the one who was wrong. I was brought up to give in! "The wiser one gives in!" was a constant remark from my mother when we siblings quarreled.

I finally left my first husband with the help of my family. And then I had the good fortune to marry a man who adored me and called me 'His Queen' and treated me as if I were one. It was a revelation I cannot even describe. I learned that I had no reason to be ashamed, on the contrary. He was so proud of me. He told me I was so easy to live with. (No wonder, as I had spend the first part of my life trying to please the closest persons in my life, whether they were nice to me or not.)

My dear late husband of 30 years spoiled me every way he knew how to, and we had a marriage 'made in heaven'.

So I have learned that there are good people and not so good people around. And that I should never put up with people who want to take advantage of me, have power over me, run my life in any way. I so often tried to please others and was not smart enough to be assertive and stand up for myself. But I have learned to say No.

My wonderful cousin Maren became a missionary. And her dream of a European Union became a reality. Her son is an ambassador and one of her daughters married a German diplomat. We all did well after some difficult years. Thank God that Danes and Germans can finally be friends after having fought each other on and off for a thousand years.

I have made it my business to tell any woman who will listen, to stay firm against any kind of abuse, verbal or otherwise. Did not Jesus say that if your eye offends you, tear it out; and if your hand offends you, you would do best to chop it off? Translate that to any person who treats you badly. Get them out of your life. Leave them and do not look back! Do not put up with injustice and manipulations.

I have made my own mistakes as a mother. I have never quite forgiven myself for the foolish decisions I made in my life which affected others. I often wish I had known as a mother what I knew later in life. I could have protected my children better. I still at times can get very angry and feel like cursing my mother or first husband when I remember certain situations, but then I give them my blessings instead, sometimes repeatedly. For you cannot curse and bless at the same time, it does not work.

A long time ago I wanted to learn to forgive, so I would not have to carry anger inside me. One approach was to bless instead of being angry. I started at present time and then went down the timeline and blessed everyone who had hurt me. It worked well all the way till I got to my childhood and mother. I could not spontaneously bless my mother. It was so awful that I burst into tears. I could not believe that I could not bless my own mother. So I had to practice it, and I did. I still do when I remember something that makes me angry. So not least for my own sake I say: "Bless you, Mother!"

I may have to say it many days in a row and many times a day. But it does work. And I acknowledge that my mother had many good qualities. She would write loving letters to me when I was away from home. She would give me things if she felt I needed something. She would tell us all not to be judgmental, yet she was the most judgmental person I have ever met. She was a complicated woman who tried to be good, but who had a difficult mindset. And I believe she was aware of that. I never understood her, perhaps because I do not understand jealousy.

I am forever grateful that I met and married my wonderful second husband. At a party he spotted me across the room and asked somebody to introduce us. Within a year we were married. Finally I made a good decision. Our marriage was made in Heaven.

I think we are spiritual beings having a human experience!

And I think I have learned my lessons. I am ready to move on."

Printed in the United States
By Bookmasters